Sparks & Embers

By:

Brooke St. James

Other titles available from Brooke St. James:

Another Shot:
(A Modern-Day Ruth and Boaz Story)

When Lightning Strikes

Something of a Storm (All in Good Time #1)
Someone Someday (All in Good Time #2)

Finally My Forever (Meant for Me #1)
Finally My Heart's Desire (Meant for Me #2)
Finally My Happy Ending (Meant for Me #3)

Shot by Cupid's Arrow

Dreams of Us

Meet Me in Myrtle Beach (Hunt Family #1)
Kiss Me in Carolina (Hunt Family #2)
California's Calling (Hunt Family #3)
Back to the Beach (Hunt Family #4)
It's About Time (Hunt Family #5)

Loved Bayou (Martin Family #1)
Dear California (Martin Family #2)
My One Regret (Martin Family #3)
Broken and Beautiful (Martin Family #4)
Back to the Bayou (Martin Family #5)

Almost Christmas

JFK to Dublin (Shower & Shelter Artist Collective #1)
Not Your Average Joe (Shower & Shelter Artist Collective #2)
So Much for Boundaries (Shower & Shelter Artist Collective #3)
Suddenly Starstruck (Shower & Shelter Artist Collective #4)
Love Stung (Shower & Shelter Artist Collective #5)
My American Angel (Shower & Shelter Artist Collective #6)

Summer of '65 (Bishop Family #1)
Jesse's Girl (Bishop Family #2)
Maybe Memphis (Bishop Family #3)
So Happy Together (Bishop Family #4)
My Little Gypsy (Bishop Family #5)
Malibu by Moonlight (Bishop Family #6)
The Harder They Fall (Bishop Family #7)
Come Friday (Bishop Family #8)

So This is Love (Miami Stories #1)

All In (Miami Stories #2)
Something Precious (Miami Stories #3)

The Suite Life (The Family Stone #1)
Feels Like Forever (The Family Stone #2)
Treat You Better (The Family Stone #3)
The Sweetheart of Summer Street (The Family Stone #4)
Out of Nowhere (The Family Stone #5)

Delicate Balance (The Blair Brothers #1)
Cherished (The Blair Brothers #2)
The Whole Story (The Blair Brothers #3)
Dream Chaser (Blair Brothers #4)

Mischief & Mayhem (Tanner Family #1)
Reckless & Wild (Tanner Family #2)
Heart & Soul (Tanner Family #3)
Me & Mister Everything (Tanner Family #4)
Through & Through (Tanner Family #5)
Lost & Found (Tanner Family #6)
Sparks & Embers (Tanner Family #7)

Chapter 1

Autumn Rains.

It wasn't describing the season and weather. It was my name. My mother was a hopeless romantic, and she thought Autumn Jade Rains was the loveliest name she could possibly think of.

She would have named all of her children seasons or other things that sounded nice with her married name of Rains, but I was an only child.

My parents did not have a conventional marriage. My father was the one and only Amos Rains. He was an author who wrote an award winning modern literary classic that was now required reading in most high schools. Students typically read it in the ninth or tenth grade. It was called The Sound a Soul Makes, and it was a coming of age time-travel novel, which contained a lot of social commentary. It was an instant classic, and its fame changed the trajectory of my father's life. He met and married my mother at the height of the book's success.

Kate Hanson was a brown-eyed debutante from South Carolina—a sweet, innocent, southern girl who was ten years younger than my father. Physically, they were a miss-matched couple. I had heard my mother referred to as a trophy wife more times than I cared to count.

My parents' road as a couple was a rocky one. My dad wrote ten other books in the nineties, but his debut work was by far his most successful. He made a good living as an author, but the majority of his career and his life were plagued with self-doubt, anxiety, and addiction. My father, although still alive, did not write anymore. He lived on bourbon and coffee, and he never, ever left his Los Angeles mansion.

I could only remember a handful of times growing up that I saw him in public, and his propensity to never leave the house got even more extreme when I was in high school and my mom filed for a divorce. He hadn't left his house in what must have been almost a decade. I went to visit him anytime I wanted, which worked out to be once or twice a month.

I had very little family. Aside from some aunts and cousins over in Carolina whom I didn't really know, my parents were my only close relatives. Seeing as how my mother just passed away last week, my father was now all I had left. Fortunately, I had some good friends in Los Angeles. I had a job I loved as well.

I had inherited my father's storytelling abilities and I made a good living as an author. No one took my writing as seriously as they took my dad's, but that didn't bother me because I didn't write about serious matters. My writing was uncomplicated and romantic. I guess, in that way, I was a mix between my mother and my father. Either way, I had enough personal success that I was no longer just thought of as Amos's daughter. I was a storyteller in my own right.

I didn't grow up saying I wanted to be a writer like my father. My love was kindled during an assignment I had in high school, and I never looked back. I was only seventeen when I released my first novel. My father obviously had connections in the publishing world, so I had a leg up with representation. But I put my all into it. I worked hard and wrote a lot, and when I was nineteen, I released a book called Evangeline's Wish that hit every bestseller list there was. It was a young adult fantasy novel that won the hearts of teenagers and twenty-somethings everywhere.

I was only twenty when I got a movie deal and twenty-two when the movie premiered. Evangeline's Wish released six years ago, and since then, my life had been set on its own course. That was my most successful book to date, but I had high hopes for the one I had just finished writing. It was called Magnolia Borderlands, and my agent and editor had both read it and told me it would easily translate to a movie. It would release this coming December, and I would know more about possible movie deals at that point.

So, there was my life in a nutshell. I was an only child with a reclusive father and a mother who was, as of a week ago, no longer alive. I had enough friends and had been into enough homes to know that my family life was lacking. But honestly, I didn't feel like I was missing anything. My life was the only life I knew, and compared to a lot of other people, it was a good one.

Currently, however, in this very moment, I was not doing my favorite thing. I had never enjoyed going to a lawyer's office. While I didn't have any bad experiences with lawyers, I also didn't go to them unless I had to.

I didn't see the point of today's visit, either. Dale Reinhardt, my mother's lawyer, assured me that one final in-person meeting was necessary to wrap up the loose ends of my mother's estate. Her passing was not a surprise, so she and I had worked out the details of her assets months before.

I had talked to Dale quite a bit over email recently. I was certain all of the paperwork had been handled. I was surprised when he called and asked for a final in-person meeting.

I walked into his office having no idea what to expect. Part of me thought my mother had secret millions somewhere and she had one final surprise planned for me. Dale's secretary smiled at me as I approached. She had a mirror behind her desk and I noticed my reflection in it. I didn't stare at myself, but I could easily see my dark hair hanging over my green blouse. She nodded at me and pointed to her left.

"Mister Reinhardt's expecting you," she said. "Can I get you something to drink?" she offered as I walked past.

"No thank you," I replied, heading for Dale's door.

"I've already alerted him you're here. He's expecting you. You can go right in."

I opened the door, feeling a bit like I was about to be handed a check. And since everything was grand in my imagination, it would probably be one of those big checks they award you for making a big donation or winning a golf tournament. Dale would smile and shake my hand as cameras flashed.

But then it hit me as I stepped into the door of Dale's office that the reason for this visit might be about *me* owing *him* something and not vice versa. Maybe he had called me here to pay some hidden legal fees or trick me out of something. It hit me, probably too late, that I might have made a mistake by going there without my own lawyer.

"Come in, Autumn," Dale said when he saw me walk through the door.

I smiled at him, but it was slightly guarded now that I was questioning the reason for this visit.

He came around his desk. I thought he was going to hug me at first, with the way he was looking at me, but then he reached for my hand. He shook it slowly and carefully, with two hands, regarding me with a regretful expression. Dale was tall, dark, and lanky. If he was a video game character, he would be

Waluigi. It was odd to see him being so soft and tender with me.

"I'm so sorry about your mom," he said.

"Thank you," I said.

"How are you holding up?" he asked, ushering me to my chair.

"I'm okay," I said.

"It doesn't matter if you have a year to expect it," he said. "It's never easy."

"Nope," I said, thinking about how surreal the last week had been.

"How's your dad taking it?" he asked.

I shrugged. "He's okay," I said, not feeling like saying much else.

Dale turned and walked around his desk. We were both quiet as he took a seat. He paused and looked at me with a thoughtful expression. He took a deep breath as he opened a folder that was sitting on his desk in front of him.

"I guess we'll just get down to business, Autumn," he said.

"Yes, we should," I agreed, feeling a little wary of his uncertainty.

Dale touched the unfolded piece of paper that was inside the folder. "I have a personal letter for you from your mother," he said. "It was her wish for me to wait until after the funeral to give it to you. She wanted me to wait until things had settled down."

"Okayyy," I said, nodding.

Dale handed it to me, still wearing that same uncertain, regretful face. His expression made me nervous. I reached out to take the paper from him. It was on his letterhead and it was typed in small font with my mother's name at the bottom. I assumed that I was just supposed to sit there and read it, and quite honestly, I was too curious to do anything else.

I turned the paper and blinked at the words.

My dearest,

I have come to the end of my life, and I need to tell you that I have held a secret from you. I am the only person on this earth who knows it, and I find that I cannot bear to take it to my grave. Let me say that I believe it's a secret you'd be better off not knowing. I had countless opportunities to tell you about it myself, and I never did. It is something about my past, and I did not share it because I would never want it to have an ill effect on you. I am leaving the decision up to you. If you ever want to know this secret in spite of my warning, you can contact Dale. He has more information. Please consider it thoughtfully. I love you and I'm sorry for putting you in this predicament. I just couldn't bear to take this to the grave with me. I had to give you the option to know.

With all my love,
Mom

I felt shaken and confused as I read the words. I stared into space for a moment before letting my gaze meet Dale's. He was still looking at me with that regretful expression.

"My mom didn't write this. She didn't use phrases like *ill effect* or *consider thoughtfully*."

"You're right," Dale said. "I wrote it for her. She told me what to say. She asked me to help organize her thoughts and take notes. I read it back to her to make sure they were the thoughts she wanted to convey, and she signed it."

"So, you know this secret?"

He paused for a few seconds "Y-yes."

"Tell me," I said without hesitation and maybe a little too casually.

Dale took a long, deep breath. "I will, and the information is yours if you want. I've written it all down right here in a second letter. Your mother read and signed this one, too."

He shifted his hand on the folder and I glanced downward to find an envelope with my name on it.

I reached out for it, and Dale put his palm toward me, wearing an expression that I could only categorize as pleading or beseeching.

"Autumn, now, just take a second and think about this."

"Why do you even care?" I asked, feeling confused. "You said the information was mine if I wanted it."

"And it is," he assured me.

"But you have to remember that your mother went her whole life not telling you these things. She loved you and she must have done that for a reason. Some things are just better left unsaid in life, Autumn."

"Well, she wanted to say them now," I said, pointing at the letter.

"Kind of," he said. "It's more that she didn't want to *not* say them."

"Is it just about my mom? Or is it about me too?"

Dale took a minute to think about his answer. "No, it has to do with you, too. Indirectly, I guess, but, yes."

"Then give it to me, please. I want to read it."

"I think it would be wise for you to just take a minute to think about it—a day or two."

"A day or two?" My tone was disbelieving and my expression was confused because I honestly couldn't believe he expected me to wait. As far as I was concerned, he was taking far too long to put the letter into my hand.

"Some things in life are just better left unknown, Autumn."

I held my hand between us, still waiting for him to hand me the letter. "You're scaring me by saying that, but of course I'm going to read it. There's just no way you can tell me there's a big secret that has to do with me and actually think I wouldn't want to know."

"Your mother mentioned that she thought she might tell you once you had children of your own. She thought maybe you'd better understand her point of view at that point."

"Thank you for your advice, Dale," I said. I smiled and got to my feet. "If that letter's mine, I'll take it and be on my way so I don't take up any of your time."

He stood up with it in his hand and extended it cautiously.

"Thank you," I said, taking the envelope from him. I stashed it and the first note in my purse.

"Are you not going to read it while you're here?"

"No, I'm taking it home," I said. And then I had a thought. "Why? Is it going to tell me to turn around and come back up here? Do you have a big check hiding away somewhere?"

Dale let out an uncontrollable scoff. "I wish. I really do wish, Autumn. It's not about money or anything you'd have to come back here for. This meeting is off the record. It's personal. Your mother only shared it with me because she didn't feel like she could keep it to herself or tell you directly."

"Okay, well, I appreciate you getting this to me."

Dale stared at me as if deciding what to say. "She wanted the best for you," he said.

"Thank you," I said. "I know she did."

Chapter 2

It took me forty-five minutes to drive from Dale's office to my apartment. I had plenty of time to open the letter and read it while I was stuck in gridlock traffic, but I didn't. I figured I needed to be sitting down somewhere comfortable when I read it since it was dramatic enough to require two letters and all those stern warnings.

My mind raced, thinking of possible outcomes. Several times, I came close to opening the envelope while I was on the road. Ultimately, I decided to wait until I got home. I lived in a beautiful apartment in downtown Los Angeles, and I figured it was as good a place as any to sit down and have a bomb dropped on me.

I had a good friend from college named Gina who came in from Santa Fe for my mom's funeral. She was staying at my apartment, but she was out visiting other friends today. She wasn't there when I left for Dale's, and I was sure I would still have the place to myself when I got back.

I parked in the garage and made my way up to my apartment, which was on the fifteenth floor. I was relieved when Gina was nowhere in sight. I kicked off my shoes and went straight to my bedroom. I closed the door behind me, sliding the soft leather purse off of my shoulder as I headed toward my bed.

I plopped onto the foot of my bed. My purse was next to me, but for several seconds, I didn't move to open it or look inside.

I recalled the way Dale looked at me. It almost seemed like he pitied me. The thought of it made me want to stubbornly rip open the envelope and read the letter. It probably wasn't even that big of a deal. Surely, if Mom had committed a crime, she wouldn't feel the need to tell her lawyer about it.

And I couldn't understand how it would be anything that could affect me. It crossed my mind that it could be that I was adopted, but I looked exactly like my mother and wrote exactly like my father, so there had never been any question about my genetics.

Part of me felt like it would be a rockstar move of me to take Dale's advice and let sleeping dogs lie. As I sat there, I seriously considered destroying the letter—envelope and all.

I had no way of knowing how serious this news was. I liked my life the way it was, and I didn't want to risk having it changed as a result of what I read. It took me another half-hour to work up the nerve to open the letter.

I could see at a glance that this one was longer than the first.

Autumn,
The following is a letter I, Dale Reinhardt, composed for your mother, Katherine Hanson Rains.

She shared with me the things she wanted to write to you, and I put them in my own words. On a personal note, since I might not speak with you again, I wanted to add that you are a fine young lady and a tremendous author. My wife and daughters absolutely love your books, and I feel proud to have known you and represented your mother. She was also a fine woman. It was her sincere wish that you had access to the following information. Take care and let me know if I can ever be of assistance to you, legal or otherwise.

Best,
Dale

Dearest Autumn,

I have made peace with God, and I know that there is a place waiting for me that is much better than any home I have ever known on this earth. My soul, however, cannot seem to find rest. I have held a secret in my heart for so many years that it is almost impossible for me to form the words to say it. I am going to share with you the full truth of the circumstances surrounding your birth.

That was the end of a paragraph, and I stopped reading and took a deep breath, looking away and absentmindedly staring at the painting on my bedroom wall.

Circumstances surrounding my birth.
What did that mean?

Was I adopted?

What other circumstances could there possibly be surrounding my birth?

My mind instantly went to the ultra-weird, and I wondered if I had been kidnapped from my original parents so she and dad could buy me on the black market.

My heart actually raced as a result of thinking that, but then I remembered something obvious. I have seen pictures of my mother when she was pregnant with me.

The letter was folded in half, resting in my hand which was next to me. I was scared to know what the rest of it said, but I was too curious to stop reading it.

I opened it again and found my place.

I do not know at what point in your life you decided to read this. I did want you to have access to it, but I hoped it would be when you were older. Please know that this information does not change who you are or what talents you were born with. It is devastating to me to think that your confidence personally or professionally could be shaken by this news.

"Get on with it, Mother," I said out loud.

I skimmed a few lines that seemed to be nothing but more warnings before getting to the start of a new paragraph.

Amos Rains is not your biological father.

I blinked as I read the sentence. Tears instantly rose to my eyes. I looked away from the letter for a second or two before I focused on the paper again.

Your father never officially knew the truth, but we tried for more children and could never conceive. I'm sure he put the pieces together, but we never had that conversation. It will have to be your decision whether or not you tell him, but for what it's worth, I think it would hurt him to know the truth.

As you know, your father and I had a whirlwind romance. We were married only a week after we met. Your conception was thought to have happened on our honeymoon, but the truth was that I was already expecting you when I met Amos.

I didn't plan on things happening in the way they did. I thought the timing of me meeting Amos and his instant affection toward me was a sign. I knew we could provide a loving home for you, and that was a better option to me than going to my parents and trying to raise you alone. I was afraid, and I made the best choices I thought I could under the circumstances.

One thing I can say for certain is that I love you very much and I made choices with you in my mind and my heart.

I paused and took a deep breath before staring down at the last section of letter.

I need you to promise me that you won't let this news hinder you in your writing, Autumn. You are your own person, and your own talents have been tested and proven. You have all the skills you need to have a long, flourishing career. You can do anything you put your mind to. You have proven that to us time and again. You learned from Amos in a way that has nothing to do with genetics, and you are talented and capable.

I scanned to the next paragraph.

I do know the name of your biological father. I don't know much about him. I can't promise that any attempt to contact him wouldn't be a complete waste of time. Amos, your father, the man who lovingly raised you, is a hero and a legend. If I were you, I would leave things the way they are.

With that being said, your biological father's name is Ben Tanner. I met him in Charlotte, North Carolina. He was there, watching his brother play basketball against the Charlotte Hornets. His brother was a famous basketball player who I'm sure you've heard of. His name is Ezekiel Tanner. I was competing in a college gymnastics competition in the same hotel where Ben and the team were staying. Ben and I met in the hotel lobby.

He was cool and confident, and he hung out with a bunch of professional athletes. He was tall and handsome, and he swept me off my feet. We were young and stupid. We were only together for one night, and while it might not have been the most ideal situation, he did give me the greatest gift I ever received in my whole life. He gave me you, Autumn. For that reason, I have never regretted it. Please forgive me, and know that I love you. Please know that this information does not need to change anything in your life. You are wonderful just the way you are. I love you with all my heart.

Mom

I took a deep breath, letting the letter fall to my side as I looked upward, toward the ceiling. I had been living in a dazed state lately, but this news plunged me into a whole new realm of out-of-it.

I was thrust into sea of emotions. Thoughts and memories began hitting me in such rapid succession that I felt like I was just along for the ride. I just sat there and stared at the ceiling, thinking. I wondered lots of things. I wondered why my mom did it, why she kept it a secret, and ultimately why she told me at all. I wondered what kind of man Ben Tanner was.

I had definitely heard of Ezekiel Tanner. He was a very famous basketball player. But given the circumstances and the one-night-stand nature of things, I had to question whether or not this person, Ben, was Ezekiel Tanner's brother at all. That seemed like a lie that would be told for the purposes of impressing the girl in the elevator.

I sat there for who knows how long, sorting through thoughts.

Chapter 3

"Lexington, Kentucky?" Courtney, my agent, looked at me like I had lost my mind. "Why would you need to go all the way to Kentucky? There are all kinds of horse ranches in California."

"I'm not trying to go to a ranch," I said.

"I thought you just said you wanted to go to a horse farm," she said.

She and I were at a restaurant together. It was a place we liked a lot—a small farm-to-table café that served things like avocado toast. I met Courtney once a week for lunch, and this place was on our regular rotation.

Today's lunch meeting just happened to fall on the day after I got the letter from Dale. I had been up until the middle of the night, going down internet rabbit holes to find out about Ezekiel Tanner's family. He did indeed have a brother named Ben, but I couldn't find much about him other than the fact that he was associated with an address in Philadelphia. A few of the family members had a Facebook page, but not all of them. From what I could tell, most of the family lived in Kentucky. I wasn't sure if Ben did, but I was almost positive he had a son who lived there and worked on Ezekiel Tanner's horse farm.

I had done enough research to know that if Ben Tanner was indeed my father, then I also had a brother. My heart ached when I thought about it. I had seen a picture of the whole family on the internet, and I so badly wanted to meet them and find out which one was my brother. I wanted to meet my brother even more than I wanted to meet Ben.

There was no way, however, that I would just waltz over there and proclaim that I was Ben's daughter. I would have to go over there and meet them under false pretenses without ever telling anyone who I was. That would be better for everyone involved, their family, my family, all of us.

When it came down to it, I had no way of knowing for certain if it was true or not. I believed my mother, but at this point, I didn't think it was worth disrupting any of our lives. I was, however, curious enough to pay the Tanner Farm a visit and check it out.

"Autumn," Courtney said, snapping in front of my face to get my attention. "Dang, girl, you are spaced all-the-way-out."

"Why? What'd I miss?" I asked, taking a package of crackers out of the basket on the table.

"I was asking why you had to go all the way to Kentucky for book research. They have horse ranches right here in California. You can probably book a visit where you have to help out and feed the animals and everything—so you get the full experience. I can't believe you want to go to a horse farm. That's the last thing I expected you to say. Are you writing a cowboy book? Are there horses in the

Borderlands sequel?" Courtney was obviously perplexed.

Our server came by and took our drink order, but then I looked at Courtney again. "It's not just any horse farm," I said. "I want to learn about Thoroughbreds… you know, for horse racing. Lexington's in the heart of all that. I was looking online, and I saw this one specific farm. I was wondering if Michael could pull some strings and get me a job there."

"A job?" Courtney said, looking stupefied. "What are you talking about? How long are you planning on staying there?"

"I don't know. I just want to have enough time to learn a few things."

"Yeah, I get that, but you can do that without pretending to have a job, Autumn. Just let me tell them who you are. I'm sure they'd be more than happy to let you go there and inspect the place. I don't think you have to go quite so far as getting a fake job." Her shock and disbelief turned into something else. She had become cautious, like maybe she was suddenly worried about me. "Are you doing okay?"

"Yeah. I've just already worked all this out in my head. I want to go there undercover. I don't want to tell them who I am. I was thinking I'd go by my initials. A.J.'s a cool name."

"You want to be called by a different name, and you want to get a job on a horse farm? A real job? Where you work?"

"Yes. I work now, Courtney."

"I know. But not on a horse farm." Courtney stared at me, unable to understand. "Why?"

"Because I want the full experience."

I was telling the truth, I did want the full experience. Courtney had no way of knowing that this trip had nothing to do with a book. Unless something hit me while I was there, I had no plans on writing about horses or horse farms at all. I would explain that later. For now, I would get to Lexington any way I could.

"Well, gosh, Autumn. You know your wish is my command... sort of... but I didn't expect this one. I'll have to talk to Michael. I don't know if he knows anyone in Kentucky."

"He knows everyone, everywhere," I said. "And he'll probably know the exact farm I'm talking about. Ezekiel Tanner owns it."

"The basketball player?" Her face was again confused.

"Yes," I said. "The basketball player. The six-foot-seven center for the Detroit Pistons. He's married with grown sons. He owns a thriving Thoroughbred horse farm in Lexington. His horses are good. They're Kentucky Derby winners and stuff."

"Oh my gosh, you did research already?"

I nodded easily since doing research was a completely normal thing for me to do.

Our server came back with our drinks, and we paused for a minute and ordered our food before beginning our conversation again.

"It's not at all what I expected to hear from you at lunch today," she said. "I'm not even quite sure what you're asking me. Do you want me to ask Michael if he can pull strings to get you a job shoveling horse junk?"

"Kind of," I said. "Or a different job on the farm."

"How long are you trying to stay over there?" she asked.

I shrugged. "A week or two."

"Oh my gosh, are you serious? Why don't you just go as a guest? Tell them you're writing an article."

"I'm not telling them I'm writing anything. Can we just set me up with some temp job for a week or two?"

"Are you trying to be a secretary? Because I know you're not going to try to pretend you can put on a horseshoe or something."

I laughed. "I'm not going to try to shoe a horse," I said. "And it's a big farm. I don't see why I can't just fly under the radar with a cleaning service or something."

"I'll see what I can do. I'll talk to Michael. This seems like a tall order, though. When are you trying to do this?" she asked.

"Soon. Next week."

"Next week? I thought you had company in town. I thought you'd want to take a little time off."

I didn't know whether she was referring to the fact that I had recently completed a book or if she was referring to my mom passing away. Either way, it was weird for Courtney to encourage me to take time off, so I just shrugged and shook my head.

"I do have company, but she's leaving tomorrow. And I'm fine," I added. "I think it'd be worse for me to sit around and do nothing. I'm not diving into anything right away, but I do want to get this research done—make some notes."

"Are you trying to write about Ezekiel Tanner?" she asked. "If he's married and has hot kids, it could be an epic but true love story."

"I don't do biographies."

"I don't mean literally him. I'm just saying, he'd probably be pretty good inspiration. You could have a love story with famous athletes and racehorses."

I laughed and shook my head. "I'm not writing whatever you just said," I said, eating a whole cracker in one bite. "I'm not even listening to you right now. You know I don't tell you my plans, anyway."

"Fine," Courtney said, acting mad even though she wasn't at all. "I'll ask Michael to try to get my number one client a fake job cleaning up horse junk at Ezekiel Tanner's farm."

"Thank you," I said.

Courtney was the best. She called me the following day with information about my new job. "It's a company called Pleasant Landscaping," she said. "They have a crew at the Tanner Farm three days a week. Monday, Wednesday, Friday. Michael said they'd give you a shirt and a hat, and basically you just need to make yourself look busy and stay out of their way. They might have you pull weeds or something. The owner knows who you are, but the workers think it's a temporary job for you. Michael told the owner to call you A.J., like you wanted."

I started to be bummed that the owner knew I was a writer or that I would only be able to go to their house three days a week, but then I remembered how amazing it was that I could say the word and get a fake job at a specific horse farm.

"Thank you," I said. "Thanks for taking care of that. It sounds perfect."

"I also got hotel reservations. It's not a huge city but there were a few nice places downtown."

"Sounds perfect. You're amazing. When do I leave?"

"I think it's like nine or ten days from now. That landscaping place is expecting you to show up on a Monday, so I got your flight and reservation set up for the Sunday before. I rented you a car and everything. It'll be at the airport."

"How long did you tell them I'd be there?" I asked.

"Two weeks," she said. "Six days of tagging along with that landscaping company. I don't know how helpful they'll be or how much information you'll get, but you'll figure it out, I guess."

"Yes, I will. And it's perfect. Thank you. I love you."

It was normal for Courtney and I to say I love you, and she answered back without hesitation.

"I love you too."

Chapter 4

Ten days later

I stared out of the window from the back seat of a pickup truck, wondering what in the world I had gotten myself into. I set an alarm for an ungodly hour so that I could get dressed and meet the crew from the landscaping place at 7am.

I had been up for over an hour, and I was relatively sure that it was only 4am in Los Angeles, so it was no wonder I was out-of-it. It might have been good that I was a little dazed because I had never been so nervous in all my life.

In my fantasy, I would encounter my long-lost brother the instant I got to the farm. I would accidently meet him the second I set foot on the property. We would have a pleasant, witty exchange. I would be able to evaluate, just by looking at him, the probability of us sharing the same father.

The truth was that I wasn't even sure if my brother would be there at all. All I knew (and I wasn't even sure about this) was that he lived in Lexington.

I was currently riding in a truck with three guys. I had been there when Jesse, the owner of Pleasant, gave the three-man crew the rundown about me. He introduced me and told them that I would be willing to do some easy work tasks, but that they should take it easy on me. I could tell, just from Jesse's slightly nervous demeanor and willingness to please me that he was a little starstruck. Michael had probably told him everything. I was sure he had dropped my name and probably my father's in order to make this happen.

Jesse called me A.J., which was a little weird, since I knew he knew who I was. He mentioned to the crew that I was just temporary, but they were no nonsense guys who just wanted to get to work. They didn't question it or really seem to care that I was going with them.

"I'll have you helping Nick and Tyson with the flowerbeds at one of the stables," said the guy in the driver's seat. I was pretty sure his name was Dan.

"Sure," I said, nodding and agreeing easily.

"I see you didn't bring water," said Nick, the guy sitting next to me. He looked all around me as if searching for some source of water.

"I didn't," I said. "Is that bad?"

"We have a cooler on the truck," he said. "But there aren't any cups. You just have to stick your head under it and let the water fall into your mouth."

"We'll be at the big stables," the driver said. "There's a kitchen and bathroom and everything. She'll be fine."

"Do you guys work at the Tanner Farm all the time?"

"Yep," Nick said. "Dan's been working there for like six years." He gestured at the driver.

"Six years?" I asked. "Every day?"

"Every day," Dan said. "I'm full-time with the Tanners no matter what season it is. In the summer, I have a small crew with me every day. We just went to our fall schedule, so these guys come with me three times a week now. I'll do that for a few months, and then, in the winter I come by myself. But there's always something for me to do. I never have idle time. Their property is enormous. They have a guy who does nothing but paint. Between the fence and all the structures, he just paints full-time."

"They have a full-time painter?" Nick asked, sounding amazed.

"Yes," Dan said, nodding. "They need it, believe me."

"Have you seen the farm?" Nick asked, looking at me.

"No, I haven't."

"Well, now you have," Dan said.

I looked at him and he gestured out the window. I stared out to find beautiful, tree-lined pastures. As far as I could see, there was that same type of fence that ran lengthwise and was all over Lexington. The property we were on now had white double fencing, which was gorgeous. It looked like every beautiful image of Kentucky I searched on the internet. I couldn't believe the man who lived there could be my uncle.

"Oh my gosh," I muttered.

It was more of a… *what have I gotten myself into*, but Dan said, "It's amazing, isn't it?"

"You know who it is who lives here, don't you?" Nick asked.

I nodded. "Ezekiel Tanner."

"Do you like basketball?" Tyson asked, turning around from the front seat.

I nodded. "I didn't grow up in a big sports family, but if I were to go to a sporting event, it would probably be basketball."

"Ezekiel's awesome," Dan said. "He's way more down-to-earth than you'd expect. You'll probably get to meet him. He's around the farm a lot." Dan turned onto a private road, and I got even more nervous than before.

As it turned out, there was no time for nerves. The fine gentlemen at Pleasant Landscaping were not there to play around. Before I knew it, we had parked at the stables and went straight to work. Nick, Tyson, and I were tasked with pulling weeds in the flowerbeds before mulch could be spread. There weren't an overwhelming number of weeds, but the flowerbeds were huge, and we had to walk around, checking them all, and pulling anything that didn't belong.

It wasn't a mentally difficult job, but it was physically demanding, and I wasn't used to all the squatting. I had to pace myself and go slower than the guys. We did that for over an hour before Tyson and Nick started hauling bags of mulch off of the trailer. I offered to fall in line and help them, but Dan said they had a system that I'd be better off waiting until they were ready to open the bags and spread it.

And spread it was exactly what we did. I opened and spread bag after bag of cedar mulch. I was relatively sure that the smell of cedar would be in my nostrils for the rest of my life. I worked for two hours straight before Dan came over to check on me. I had been working on the side of the stables, and he was amazed by how much I had done.

"Did you do all that?" he asked, gesturing to the flowerbed.

I nodded, standing up and wiping at my face with the back of my forearm.

Dan laughed. "Dang girl, you better pace yourself," he said. "You keep working like this, and I'll have to get you trained on the bobcat."

I laughed, even though I had no idea what he was talking about.

"There's a kitchen in the stables," he said. "I'll show you where it is and you can go in there and take a little break."

I had gotten so into the task of spreading mulch that it took me a second to remember that I was there for other reasons. I instantly agreed to take a break, and just like that, we began walking toward the front of the stables. It was a gorgeous Spanish-inspired structure, and I looked all around as we walked.

Dan turned to go through an open doorway, and I followed him. Neither of us felt the need to fill the silence with talking. He seemed to be a quiet guy, and I was doing enough thinking for the both of us.

"These are apartments," he said, tapping the expansive stucco wall on his right as we walked. "Do you mean for people, or is that what they call it for horses, too?"

Dan laughed. "For people. They're actually really nice. Simple, one-bedroom apartments, but they're nice. It's the groom's quarters."

"Who lives there? Grooms, I assume?"

"Not always. It's changed over the years. There are a few of them here, and a couple more over at a different barn. Usually, it's people who work here— a groom or stable manager. Mister Tanner's nephew lived in one of them for years, and now a friend of their family does. It just depends."

"I guess it would be cool to be a nephew of Ezekiel Tanner."

Dan chuckled. "It would be extremely cool," he agreed.

We continued down the wide walkway until finally, I started seeing the compartments with horses. None of them had their heads sticking out, but as we passed each compartment, I could see that horses were in most of them. There was a certain mixture of smells in the stables. It wasn't bad. It smelled like horses and hay and dirt and leather. I made a mental note to take some allergy medicine when I got back to the hotel.

I wanted to ask more about Ezekiel Tanner's nephew, but I wasn't sure how to bring it up. "Does he still live there? Mr. Tanner's nephew?"

Dan had already clarified that he didn't, but I couldn't drop the subject, so I went ahead and asked. "Who, Jude? No. He's married now. But he's here all the time. He works here, and he and his wife have a house on the farm."

"This farm?" I asked.

"Yeah. Mister Tanner gave land to his boys. They all have houses on the property. We don't take care of any of that, though. Pleasant does, but not me. They have their own contracts that I'm not a part of." I was confused. I thought we had been talking about Mr. Tanner's nephew, but Dan just said he *gave land to his boys,* which made me think we were talking about his sons.

"Here we are," Dan said, gesturing to a door. He opened it, and we walked inside. It was cool and inviting, and there was no one else in there.

"Jesse made me promise not to over work you," he said. "He'd kill me if you quit after the first day. Just take your time and rest for a little while, and when you're ready to get back to it, come see me and we can figure out another job."

"I wasn't even halfway done with that mulch on the side," I said.

He smiled. "Tyson will finish it."

"Did I not do it right?"

"Oh, no, you did great. I just didn't know you were going to work so hard. Like I said, Jesse told me to take it easy on you." Before I could say anything, Dan spoke again. "I saw that you didn't bring any lunch today."

"Was I supposed to?"

"We always do. We only work until two, so we usually just take a half-hour and sit in the truck to eat. I have an extra sandwich if you want it. I'll grab it for you if you want to sit in here and eat it."

"No, no, no, no, I'm totally fine waiting until two o'clock to eat. I'll go get something on my way back to the—back home."

"Are you sure?" Dan asked, hesitating. "I don't mind. My wife makes me two sandwiches every day. Half-the-time, I give one to Tyson."

He barely had time to finish a sentence when someone walked through the door. He was a massive man. Based on his size, my instant thought was that he was Ezekiel Tanner, but once I focused on his face, I realized he was much younger.

I gazed at him and smiled blankly. I was trying to remember all the pictures I had seen on the internet—trying to figure out if this guy was family. He must be. *Was he my brother?* He was really handsome. I would be proud to have a guy like this for my brother. I felt hot liquid start to well in my eyes at the thought, and I bent down and pretended to tie my shoe. Of course, I didn't just pretend to do

it since they were both standing there looking at me.
I untied it and tied it again as if it needed adjusting. I
didn't think they were paying attention to me,
anyway. I heard them talk to each other.

"How's it going, Dan?" the guy asked.

"Good. Great. How are you?"

"Fine."

The guy had a deep voice to match his stature.
He wasn't just tall, he was also big. He wasn't lanky.
He was stout and sturdy. He had a trim build and he
was fit, but there was a certain thickness to him that
made me feel delicate by comparison. I rarely saw
men this size in real life—his stature was the stuff of
fiction. Of course, I didn't hang out with basketball
people too much, so maybe they all looked like this.
Could he be my bother?

"This is A.J.," Dan said. "She's working with us
now."

"Hello A.J.," said the giant of a man.

I wanted to cry.

That name sounded like a lie.

I wanted him to call me Autumn.

What had I been thinking, changing my name?

"Hello," I said, performing an awkward little
wave.

He locked eyes with me, and our gazes held for
several seconds. He had dark eyes and hair like me. I
tried desperately in those seconds to search his eyes,
but I couldn't tell whether or not I felt like I was

related to him. I didn't know what I felt. It was a surreal situation.

"All right, A.J., I'm heading out," Dan said, breaking the silence. "Are you all right in here?"

"Yes. Fine. Thank you. I'll just take a minute."

"Are you sure about that sandwich?"

"Positive," I said. "I'm not hungry at all."

"Okay, take your time," he said on his way out. "See you, Alex."

"See you," the tall guy returned.

Alex. Alex. *Who was Alex? Was he Ben's son?*

"Are you Ezekiel Tanner's son?" I asked, as soon as Dan left the room. I cringed inwardly at myself for being so blunt, but he didn't seem fazed. He smiled from over his shoulder as he reached into the cabinet for a plate.

"No," he replied. "But he's like a father to me."

My heart began to race.

I began tripping over my words. "N-nephew? Are you his—so, are you his nephew, then? Y-you said he was *like a father*."

Goodness, Autumn. I clamped my mouth shut and waited for him to answer.

"No, I'm not. I'm not related to the Tanner's at all. Technically, anyway. They're like family. They treat me like I'm one of them. I went to school with Jordan. We played basketball together at UK. I'm Alex Holbrook."

"Nice to meet you," I said, taking a seat at one of the tables in the middle of the room. I felt simultaneously relieved and disappointed.

Alex pulled a platter out of the fridge and set it on the counter.

"So, do you just come over to their farm to eat lunch? To the stables? I thought they had a house."

Alex laughed a little. "They do have a house. The big house. And they wouldn't mind if I went over there to dig in their fridge. But Allison brought this over from the restaurant where she works, and she texted and let us all know." Alex paused and pulled back the foil, smiling as he stared at its contents. "Yeah, it'd be a shame to see this go to waste. It's pasta. It's got steak mixed in. Are you sure you don't want some of it?"

"Do all the w-workers get to eat? Just get food out of their fridge?" I stuttered, and Alex's face broke into a wide grin, and I had to look away. His face was so handsome and he carried himself differently, more confident and masculine than most of the guys I came in contact with back home.

"There is plenty of food here," he said. "Why don't you let me make you a plate."

"Okay," I said, smiling at him. By that time, I could see the pasta. I didn't realize I was hungry, but it looked delicious.

"Okay," he said. "Great. You won't be sorry."

Chapter 5

"If you don't mind, just rinse the dishes when you're done and put them in the dishwasher." Alex set the plate of pasta in front of me as he made that statement, and I looked up at him. I expected him to sit at the table with me, but he was standing and holding his plate like he was poised to leave.

"Where are you going?" I asked.

"I was going... back to my apartment. I usually... just... eat over there." His answer came out sounding slightly stiff like he was hesitating.

I gave him a confused expression. "Why did you even heat it up if you're just going to leave? It's going to be cold by the time you get home."

He grinned. "My apartment's right there, but..." he trailed off as he stepped toward me and found a seat at my table. He set his plate down across the corner from me. "You want some water?" he asked.

"No, this is great."

"Are you sure? I'm getting myself some, anyway."

He crossed to the kitchen, presumably to get a glass for water.

"You don't have to stay," I said. "I didn't know you... where do you live?"

"Right over there. There are apartments built into these stables."

"Dan was telling me about those," I said. "I just didn't know you lived in one of them."

Alex glanced at me with a smile as he poured water from the free-standing water cooler next to the fridge. "How would you?" he asked, teasing me.

"Do you work here?" I asked, clearing my throat. "No. I just live here. The apartment came up empty when Jude moved out. I was in grad school, and barely making ends meet, and well, like I said, the Tanners treat me like family."

He set two glasses of water on the table and sat in a chair.

"Thank you," I said.

My heart began pounding at the mention of Jude because I thought that might be my brother's name. I forced myself to ignore it.

"This looks delicious," I said as I took a small bite. It was steak and cheese pasta, and it was amazing. "What's the rent like in a stable apartment?" I asked, trying to get my mind off of Jude.

"It's free, for me," he said.

"You get to live here for free?" I asked. "Is your apartment nice?"

"It is, and I do," he said. "I help the Tanners out when I can, but they're extremely generous with me. They always have been. I owe them a lot. Ezekiel Tanner has been like a father..." Alex trailed off, smiling and nudging his chin toward the door. I looked that way. Ezekiel Tanner, the man himself, was standing there. He looked to be about the same size as Alex. Maybe even a little taller. He smiled as he walked in. I didn't know many athletes in the world, but you can't go through life and not know about Ezekiel Tanner. I felt starstruck, speechless.

"I'm sorry to interrupt you two," he said, walking in and not skipping a beat. "But I couldn't help but overhear as I came in. Do not let this boy tell you he owes us anything. He does way more for us than his rent is worth. Plus, we love having him here." Ezekiel crossed to the fridge and took out the tray of pasta. "I didn't know you were entertaining a lady friend for lunch, Alex. I'll heat up my plate and get out of y'all's way."

"Oh, I'm not… I'm just… I'm actually here with Pleasant." I pointed to the logo on my company t-shirt. "You know, lawn care. Dan. I'm with Dan. He told me I could sit in this kitchen to catch my breath, and Alex just offered me a—"

"A.J.'s working with Dan today," Alex explained. "She was in here taking a break, and I made her a plate of pasta."

"Hello, there, Miss A.J. I'm glad you're eating some of this. It's good stuff. I told Jordan and Logan it was in here, but I'm not sure if they'll come over and get some."

Ezekiel went about the business of making his plate, whistling. And while he was busy, I focused on Alex again. "How long have you lived here?" I asked.

"About three years," he answered. "I had a different apartment when I was doing my undergraduate degree, but it was part of my basketball scholarship. I wasn't allowed to have a job during grad school, and I didn't have my scholarship anymore, so things got tight. At first, I was just going to stay until I finished my doctorate, but that happened a year ago. I'm working now, and I could afford my own place, but, I mean, come on... they've got me spoiled." I looked at him to find that he was smiling and holding his hands up, motioning to our surroundings.

"We want Alex to stay here as long as he will," Ezekiel said from across the room. "He'll tell you he doesn't pay rent, but between all the PT work he does for our family, I'm sure it's us who owe him by now and not the other way around."

"I assure you it's the other way around," Alex said, looking at me dryly.

I smiled at him. He was sweet and humble for such a big brute.

Ezekiel took his food out of the microwave and came to sit next to us. "I'm going to crash your party now that I know you're not on a date," he said, settling in a chair at our table.

"Please do," I said. I was nervous, but they were easy-going enough guys that I was able to relax and eat and act like my normal self. "You're going to have to tell me about this work Alex does. You said PT, but I got tripped up on that. I'm afraid I don't know what that means. Is it something to do with horses, I assume?"

"No, no, no," Ezekiel said. "Physical therapy. He's a physical therapist. You know, for muscles and stuff. He's good. He's full-time at the university with their athletic department." Ezekiel smiled at Alex. "And then he comes home, and we call him with all our aches and pains over here, too."

I glanced at Alex who smiled. "I love my work," he said. "I'm happy to help when I can."

"It's amazing what physical therapy can do," Ezekiel said. "And Alex is smart. He's got a real understanding of the body and how things are connected. Have you ever had to have it?" Ezekiel took a big bite of his food, and then he looked at me as if waiting for my answer. I couldn't believe Ezekiel Tanner was just sitting across from me, chewing food like a normal person.

"Yeah, I did have to have physical therapy once. I sprained my ankle when I went hiking this one time, and took forever to get better. It was making me walk funny, and I ended up tweaking my back because of it. I went to a physical therapist for that. He gave me some exercises to do for my leg and my back, actually."

"Did it help?" Alex asked.

"Yeah, it did. It got better. Is that what physical therapy is most of the time? Exercising with those bands and stuff?"

"It is," Alex said. "The trick is figuring out what movements and exercises your body needs to counteract the pain or immobility. You have to know a lot about the body—how it's all connected. That's why PT school is so intense."

"Alex got his doctorate in three years. He's one of the hardest working guys I've ever met, and that's saying a lot considering the people I've been around in my life."

Alex looked at me. "This is exactly why I'll be living in a one-bedroom apartment in the stables for the rest of my life."

Ezekiel took a big bite of pasta and was still chewing when he put his hand on Alex's shoulder. "I told Rhonda I was gonna wait till your birthday, but you're making it impossible." He swallowed and took a breath, hesitating a little. "Don't even think about telling her I told you this… but you know that lot on the other side of Jude's… that's yours. We know you're saving for a down payment on a house, and we were hoping you would want to just build out here on that lot."

Alex said nothing. He stared at his food. His eyes were so far open that I could easily see that he was working hard to hold back tears. He blinked. No tears escaped, but his eyes were glassy. His jaw clinched for a second before he spoke.

"I don't know if you're serious, or—"

"I'm completely serious," Ezekiel said. "Rhonda and I already talked to the lawyer and told him we wanted to put that lot under your name. If you want it, of course. It'd be a couple of acres past that tree line, over by Jude's. You know where I'm talking about. You'd be on that back access road. We would love it if you decide to stay. There's no question that you're going to outgrow that apartment, and we weren't looking forward to seeing you go."

I felt like I was invading their privacy—like I was present at a sincere, possibly life-changing moment. Alex had stopped eating, but he still stared at the table. I knew, just from first impressions, that he was comfortable with eye contact. But right then, he was staring into space. He was hiding his emotions, but I could just tell by the way he stared that he was overwhelmed.

I felt overwhelmed just looking at him.

His situation hit home for me.

Alex was an outsider who had been taken in by the Tanner family, and that resonated with me, making me feel like I wanted to cry, too. My jaw began to ache, and I just sat there, trying not to think about this sweet moment or the fact that it somehow, in some indirect way, maybe applied to me.

You're reading too much into it.

That was what I told myself as a means of distraction.

"Did you mention this to Jordan?" Alex asked.

"It was Jordan's idea," Ezekiel said. "Well, him and his mama cooked it up."

"I don't even know what to say," Alex said. His tone was sincere as he stared at Ezekiel.

"Say you'll stay," Ezekiel said.

"I'll stay," Alex said somewhat dazedly. "I'll definitely stay."

Ezekiel grinned. "Good. It's decided, then." "We'll work out the details later. Please don't tell Miss Rhonda I told you. She'd wring my neck. I don't even know why I did that. I'm going to be in so much trouble if she finds out. She wanted to save it for your birthday. When's your birthday? Next month?"

"Yes sir."

Ezekiel nodded. "Yeah, please just don't mention it."

"I promise I won't," Alex said. "I can hardly believe it much less talk about it."

Ezekiel smiled. "You better believe it, because it's yours. It'll be your land and obviously whatever house you build on it. It's yours unless you go to sell it. If you want to sell it for any reason, down the road, I only ask that you sell it back to me. I'll pay you what it's worth, but I don't want it going to anyone else. It'll be yours though, as long as you want it."

I ate a bite of my food. I had to swallow against the lump in my throat.

"I—uh—thank you, Ezekiel" Alex said. "Thank you is not enough, but thank you. I'm so happy right now, I can't even react." Alex took a deep breath and tensed up, leaning back in his chair stiffly like he just couldn't contain his excitement.

"When did you get into landscaping, Miss A.J.?" Ezekiel was the one who asked the question, and I smiled at him as I swallowed a bite of food.

"I'm a beginner. Today's my first day."

"Really?" he said, looking surprised.

I nodded. "Really."

I was nervous. I was a fairly good liar, but I didn't like doing it, so I decided to be as honest as I could.

"Well, it's good you're working with Dan," Ezekiel said. "He knows his stuff. You can learn a lot from him."

I smiled and nodded. "And it's a good workout. I was working at a desk before this, so there wasn't much muscle involved."

"You have to balance it out on the weekend, that's what they say. Switch it up on the Sabbath."

"What do you mean?" I asked.

"You know, if you spend your work week sitting in a chair, using your mind, then you need to use your muscles and get dirty on the weekend. If you use your muscles and get dirty for a job, then you need to sit in a chair and use your mind on the weekend."

"That's pretty good," I said. "I've never heard that. Who says that? Tony Robbins? Doctor Oz?"

They laughed.

"I don't know where I heard it," Ezekiel said.

"I'm only working Monday, Wednesday, and Friday with Dan."

"That's right, he's by himself Tuesday and Thursday. I forgot it was September already. Are you going to work somewhere else Tuesday and Thursday?"

"No, I'm just three days with the landscaping place for now. Part-time, I guess."

We were all eating while having the conversation, so we were speaking slowly and casually.

"Did you grow up in Lexington?" Alex asked.

"No. California, actually. I just moved over here."

"Really? Welcome," Ezekiel said, sounding sincere. "You're going to love Kentucky."

"Thank you," I said. "It's beautiful here, and the people are really nice so far."

"What brought you to Lexington?" Alex asked.

"I… just… wanted a… change of pace, I guess."

It was the best I could do. I had no idea these people would be so friendly, so interested in a random landscaper girl.

Chapter 6

I sat and shared an enjoyable lunch with Alex and Ezekiel.

I felt I had no other choice but to take over the conversation. I asked about the pasta we were eating, and then I started asking questions about physical therapy and horse farming. Both of them were charming gentlemen. They were tough and masculine, but also smart and quick-witted.

I found myself feeling attracted to Alex. It wasn't physical. I mean, it was. I was attracted to him physically. *How could I not be?* But my attraction wasn't about that. I had too much going on in my mind to worry about impressing a guy. I was attracted to him for other reasons. Part of me felt like he and I were equals. He was an outsider who the Tanners had taken in. And while I didn't think I would ever be in his exact shoes, living on the property, it was a relief to know that they were kind, generous people.

We sat in that kitchen and talked for about a half-hour before Ezekiel got to his feet. "Y'all stay," he said, as he stood up. "I think I'll get a little of this pasta and take it to the house for Rhonda and be out of your way. It was nice meeting you, A.J."

"It was nice meeting you, too," I said. I sat up on the edge of my chair like I was about to stand up, but Ezekiel was already moving toward the sink, so I relaxed a little, looking at Alex. "Thank you for lunch," I said.

"You're welcome," he replied. "But all I did was put it on a plate."

"Well, that was the only way it could have gotten in my stomach, so thank you."

He grinned. "You're welcome."

"I'll wash our plates so you can get back to work," I said. He told me during our conversation earlier that he got to come home for lunch just about every day, so I figured he needed to think about getting back to the college.

His short hair was just a little longer on top, and he ran his hand through it, pushing it away from his face. He had on a short-sleeved shirt, and when he picked up his arm, I couldn't help but notice the muscles on the backside of it. There was a perfect bulge lining the back of his upper arm. He was simply a big guy. His physique was quite distracting.

In my regular life, I would gawk and say, "Dang, son, how much do you work out?" But Ezekiel was still in the room, and the whole situation made me a little shy.

"I'm not going back to work until four," Alex said. "I have this part of the afternoon off, but I have to go back from four to six, during practice time, to do a session with a few of my injured football players."

"I've never been to a football practice," I said.

Alex's dark eyes met mine. He regarded me with a curious, thoughtful expression, hesitating for a second before he said, "D-did you want to come with me? We'd be outside, so you wouldn't be in anybody's way. I took a friend with me to check it out one time, and it was no big deal."

"Just so you're not working for the other team," Ezekiel said, hearing our conversation.

"Oh, no. Definitely not. I don't even know what they're doing out there."

"Good," Ezekiel said, smiling. He opened the fridge to deal with the pasta, and I focused on Alex again.

"I'll go," I said to him. "I've always been curious about football." (This was the truth. As a writer, I was curious about everything.)

"Okay," Alex said with a nod. "Would you just want to ride with me, or… meet me over there?"

"I get off at two o'clock, so I could maybe just meet you over there. I don't have my car with me here. It's at the landscaping place. I rode in the truck with the guys."

"I'll see you two later," Ezekiel said as he walked toward the door. "Nice to meet you," he said touching his hand to my back briefly.

"Nice to meet you, too," I said, glancing over my shoulder at him.

He smiled as he turned his attention to Alex. "I forgot to ask, have you seen Tanner?"

"Yes sir," Alex said. "He came by this morning."

"How's that foot?"

"It's hurting right now, but they ran tests and said it's just a sprain. I told him to come see me every day so I can keep an eye on it. He'll be out for a couple of weeks, I'm sure."

"All right, keep me posted."

"I will."

Ezekiel patted Alex's shoulder. "Thank you."

Alex looked up at him. "Thank *you*," he said.

Ezekiel smiled and gave us one last wave before walking out of the door.

"Who's Tanner?"

"Ezekiel's nephew. His sister's son. He's a senior at UK. A basketball player. He's really good. He's been starting since he was a sophomore. You probably would have heard of him if you were from here."

"How many brothers and sisters does Ezekiel have?" I asked.

"Just one of each, but his brother doesn't live here. Tanner is his sister, Sara's, son. She made his first name Tanner after her maiden name. Their last name is Wilde. Sara and Ricky Wilde. They all live here. The Tanners have a big family, with cousins and everything."

"How many kids do the Wildes have?" I asked.

"Three."

"And Ezekiel?"

"Two."

"Jordan's his younger son. He's my best friend. He's still playing in the NBA. He finished his fourth year."

"Really?" I said, even though I had read something about that. I was so happy Alex was clarifying that I was willing to act like it was the first time I heard everything. "What team?"

"The Pelicans. New Orleans."

"Oh, he lives in New Orleans?"

"Half the year."

"What about his other son?" I asked.

"Zeke lives here, on the farm. He and Jordan both have a good-sized piece of property."

"I guess you do too now, by the sound of things."

"I'm still blown away by that," Alex said, shaking his head with a serous expression. "It's so weird that he just told me that over lunch at the stable kitchen. If this is true, Miss Rhonda seriously would kill him for telling me."

"I think it's wonderful that he did it. I wouldn't have been a part of it any other time."

"Well, unless it's Monday, Wednesday, or Friday," he said, teasing me.

"Yeah, but even then, I'm only in here for like ten minutes," I said. "What are the chances that I'd be in here when he told you that?"

"They're about one in two-hundred-ten, if you factor days of the week and lunchbreak times."

"Are you being serious?" I asked.

He was straight-faced, and I stared at him with wide eyes thinking he must be some kind of genius. His face broke into a sideways amused grin and he shook his head at me. My stomach flipped at the sight of it.

"Did you just make that up?"

"Yes," he said, his grin broadening. "I do love math, but there's no way I could… I mean… I guess I could figure some kind of probability about us all running into each other, but I've known Ezekiel eight years and he's never had a conversation like that with me. So, I'd say you're right. The chances of overhearing that conversation are pretty slim."

"I'm happy I was here. That's amazing news for you. I feel like you just won the lottery right in front of me or something."

He smiled. "I feel like I won the lottery right in front of you, too. Let's go get some ice cream."

I smiled at him because he was so serious and nonchalant when he said it.

"Is that just something you say when you're happy?" I asked. "Or are you really asking me to go for ice cream?"

"I'm really asking you. I guess it's something I say when I'm happy, too, but I was really asking you to get ice cream with me." He shrugged.

"When would we do that?"

"After dinner?"

"Right now?" I asked. "Do you call lunch dinner and dinner supper? They do that in the south."

"No, I call dinner-dinner. I'm from Iowa."

I tilted my head at him. "Are you asking me to dinner tonight?"

"I usually don't eat ice cream before real food," he said. "I figured we would need to get dinner first if we're going to get ice cream. Just… logically."

"And when is this supposed to happen?" I asked.

"You'll already be with me after practice at six o'clock tonight. That's dinner time. Seems reasonable to roll with it."

I grinned. "You're a pretty reasonable guy, aren't you?"

"I take that as a compliment, so I guess that means I am."

I shrugged. "Well I'm not going to argue reason," I said. "If it makes the most sense for us to have dinner and ice cream after football practice, then I guess that's what we should do."

Our conversation was light and jovial, but our eyes were locked on each other and there was definitely a hint of challenge to our expressions and tone. I liked Alex. He was dry witted and funny.

"I'm glad we had this talk," he said, standing up. He took my plate, but before I could thank him, he began speaking. "I could pick you up if you want," he said, taking me by surprise. "Otherwise, we'll just be following each other every time we go somewhere. You need to walk into practice with me, anyway."

"I'm okay with following each other," I said, not wanting him to pick me up at my hotel. "And I'll get there early and meet you wherever so that we can walk in on time."

"Was the ride too much?" he asked. "Starting to smell like a date?"

"Yeah, my boyfriend would be mad."

"You have a boyfriend?" he asked furrowing his eyebrows.

"No," I said, still holding eye contact, being playful.

"Oh, dang. I was hoping you did. It would make this a lot less awkward since I have a girlfriend."

"You have a girlfriend?" I asked, my heart dropping.

"No."

"You're messing with me?"

"Yes. You messed with me first, though."

"I don't have a boyfriend, and I don't mind if you think it's a date. I just don't want to ride with you."

"Fine," he said with a nod. He turned and started toward the other side of the kitchen to take our plates to the sink.

I got up and followed him over there. I could see it was customary to clean up your mess in this kitchen, and I didn't want Alex to take care of mine.

"I can get it," I said as I caught up to him.

Alex went to the sink, and I came to stand next to him, shoulder-to-shoulder. With our size difference, it was more shoulder-to-arm. He was a foot taller than me, and I had on hiking boots.

"I don't want you to wash my plate," I said. I bumped into him to try to get him to stop washing, but it was no use—I just bounced off of him. He was like a brick wall. I had read books where guys were described as a brick wall. I had even used the phrase to describe one of my own scenes. But when I imagined that character, I did not imagine him like this. Alex was seriously like a brick wall. He was huge and hard, and I just bounced off of him like a rubber ball on a brick wall.

"Don't hurt yourself," he said, glancing at me with a teasing grin.

"Don't hurt *yourself* when you… try to… race me later tonight."

His personality was just so playful that I felt like talking smack to him. I hadn't actually thought through what I was saying, though. For a second, I thought I could beat him at a foot race because I was smaller and more nimble, but then I realized I'd probably lose miserably to this guy. He was an athlete and his stride was probably twice as long as mine.

He laughed. "Please don't tell me you just challenged me to a race."

"Well, yeah, but I didn't say what kind of race," I said. "What if it's first one to find a word in the dictionary?"

"You mean first one to Google a word on your phone?" he asked. "I'll easily beat you at that. I type like lightning with these fat fingers. You wouldn't think it, but I do."

"I don't mean Google," I said. "I mean look up a word in a paper dictionary."

"What's that?" he asked. His face was serious, but I knew by now that he was joking around.

"I can tell by your scared face that I will totally destroy you at a paper-dictionary-find-a-word-race," I said.

He smirked at me. "The better trick would be to find a paper dictionary."

"I have three of them," I challenged.

"I suppose you have a thesaurus, too."

I scoffed. "I have at least one of those… on me at all times."

"You're joking."

"Am I? You'd have to check my purse."

"Is there a thesaurus in your purse?" he asked, tilting his head at me like he was genuinely curious.

"There actually is."

He shook his head at me. Our banter was relaxed and familiar, and it felt a lot like flirting. There was a possibility that he was just this cool and playful with everyone, but what we were doing sure felt like flirting. I couldn't help it. Alex was extremely flirt-with-able. He was as flirt-worthy as they came.

Chapter 7

Alex and I exchanged phone numbers so that he could text me the address of the place where the team was practicing football.

By the time I got off work, made it to the hotel, and took a shower, I had to turn around and leave again. I showed up to the practice field fifteen minutes early so that I could make sure I was waiting to meet Alex when he got there. I parked my rented SUV and got out of it, finding a spot to stand near the entrance he described.

One or two people walked in through the gate, but I was standing far enough away that they didn't even notice me. I was only there for about five minutes before Alex pulled up. He drove a truck. It was clean, but it was a basic model and it was not brand new. I got the idea that he wasn't the type to use material possessions to impress anyone. Oddly enough, this impressed me.

We walked to the practice field together and talked for a few minutes before Alex said he needed to get started with the team. He showed me where I could sit while he worked. It was just close enough that I could clearly see their facial expressions, but it was just far enough that I couldn't make out what they were saying. He was with one other guy and they were off to the side doing what looked like a modified training regimen with five of the athletes.

They were exercising, but it wasn't nearly as intense as the athletes further down on the field with the coaches.

I tried not to stare at Alex, but it was difficult. He kept drawing my attention. He was kind and smart, I could see that just by how he visually interacted with the athletes and the other trainer. He talked to each guy individually. He poked, stretched, and prodded their muscles, and he moved around their limbs before making detailed notes on his tablet.

He handled himself like a doctor, only he took his time talking to each of them, and he was extremely nice to look at in the face. Maybe there were other doctors who took their time talking to patients and were also six-and-a-half feet tall with a boyishly handsome face, but I hadn't met any. I caught myself thinking I would fake sick if I knew a doctor who looked like this. In fact, I felt a limp coming on just looking at him.

Before I knew it, Alex wrapped-up his session and came over to where I was sitting. "I should have mentioned that you weren't stuck there," he said as he approached me.

"What's that mean?"

"I should have told you that you didn't have to sit here the whole time. You could have walked around or whatever."

I stood with a groan. "Oh, no. I was happy to sit. Believe me, the last thing I needed was to walk around right now. My legs are dead."

"What's the matter?" he asked, focusing on me in physical therapist mode.

I smiled. "I'm just out of shape," I said. "I did all that squatting and bending over today, and I'm not used to it."

I fell into stride next to him and we began making our way toward the parking lot. The other players, coaches, and trainers were still on the field. Alex and I seemed to be the only ones leaving, but no one gave us a second glance. Alex asked if I wanted to ride with him to the restaurant, and I agreed easily, saying that we could just leave my car at the school and come back for it later.

We talked about football and its most common injuries on our way to the restaurant. Alex didn't even tell me where we were going. Our conversation was so non-stop, that we were suddenly pulling into a parking lot. He brought me to a place called Burrito Time. It was a small, hole-in-the-wall restaurant, and he looked at me from the driver's seat once we parked.

"Is this okay?"

"I think so. You tell me. Is it tasty?"

"Yes," he said.

I gave him a nod. "Then, it's perfect," I said, reaching for the door.

Alex and I ordered at the register and they gave us our drinks and a number to display on our table. We sat at a small booth for two. It was close quarters, and Alex was tall, and I was almost sure that if we moved just the right way our knees would touch.

I looked at him. "I liked watching you work," I said. "I'm always intrigued by people's occupations. Yours is scientific, but it also seems fun and rewarding."

"I knew, just from working with physical therapists as an athlete, that it was something I'd enjoy. I caught myself feeling like they were lucky for having that job, and I realized that must mean I wanted it too."

"Ezekiel seemed proud of you."

"He's amazing. That whole family is just a Godsend. Literally. I think God actually sent them to me. I might have lived through grad school without them, but it would not have been pretty. They refused to take money for rent or utilities, and Miss Rhonda is always feeding me and dropping off things at my apartment like laundry or dish detergent. She's seriously like a mom to me, which is different. I wasn't used to that. I wasn't raised with a mom like that."

"I thought you said you grew up with a mom."

"I did. I was. My mom was single. She was busy with work, and she was trying... I don't know... I guess she was just busy trying to get guys to notice her. I didn't know what was happening at the time, but looking back, I think she wanted guys who were out of her league so she just kept jumping around to different men and getting her heart broken. She was just distracted a lot. I took care of my little brothers the best I could, but they weren't that much younger than me, so we were all kind of in it together. By the time I was going off to college, they kind of started making their own choices in life. They're both still back in Iowa. I have family back there, but I also spent a lot of time alone. My teammates… my basketball family was more who I went with, even back then. That took on a whole new meaning once I got over here to UK and met Jordan. I don't even know how I got so close to them. Jordan just… started inviting me places. First, I was eating meals over there and then I was doing Christmas and Thanksgiving, and all the other family stuff."

"So, is it just Ezekiel's kids, or is it all… all the cousins and everything?"

"Yeah, it's cousins, aunts, uncles, grandparents. There's a lot of them, between the Tanners and Wildes."

"Does Ezekiel have a brother… Ben?"

Apparently, I couldn't pass up the opportunity to mention it, because the question popped out of my mouth before I could think better of it. I instantly picked up my glass and took a sip out of the straw, just to have something to do with my hands and mouth.

"He does. Ben lives out of state and so does his daughter, but Jude lives here. Ben's son."

"Oh, Jude? Is he around much?" I asked.

My stomach dropped even as that name came out of my mouth. *I was being too obvious.*

"Jude? Yeah, he's around all the time. He's the one we were talking about today when E was telling me where that lot was. He and his wife, Andy, have a piece of land on the edge of the farm. We see them all the time."

"They just come to the farm, or..." I trailed off in a questioning tone. Alex was answering all of my questions, so I just kept asking them.

"Yeah, they do. Jude works there. He spends a lot of time in the stables where I met you earlier. He just had a new baby."

"He did? Him and his wife had it?"

"Yes," Alex said, chuckling. "She had the baby, but Jude's the dad. Why? Do you know him?"

"No, how would I?"

"I don't know," he said. "You were asking about him."

"No, I didn't mean to ask about him specifically. We were just talking about the Tanners, and I was just wondering about the whole family. I didn't know there were so many of them."

"Oh, yeah, there's a lot. Cousins and everything. And they're all having babies now, so there are babies all over the place, too."

"What did Jude have? You said he had a new baby. I love babies, so I was just curious."

"They had a little boy," Alex said. "He's just a month or two old. They drove down to New Orleans to introduce him to Andy's family."

"Oh… when… now? They're in New Orleans now? I thought you said Jordan lived there."

"He does, but so does Andy's family. That's where Jude is now. At least they were on Saturday. I think they still are."

I nodded like it was of no consequence to me. I wanted to ask more. I wanted a detailed report of Jude's itinerary. But Alex didn't know any of that, and besides, I had already asked way too much about Jude. Alex's willingness to be open with me made me feel like I owed him something.

"My mother passed away recently," I said.

"Oh, gosh, I'm sorry. When?"

"Three weeks ago."

"Seriously? Wow. Was that before or after you moved?"

"I was still in California," I said. "She was sick for a while, but no matter how much you expect it, it's still weird."

"I bet. And I'm sorry. I wish I knew something better to say than that."

"It's okay," I said. "I'm okay. But I know what you mean about being alone. I'm an only child and my parents were a little preoccupied like you said yours were. My mom and I got closer toward the end, but I always had a really quiet family life. My father still lives in California, but he's really all the family I have. My mom's family is from South Carolina, but I've only met them a few times."

"Are you going to try to see them, now that you're closer?"

I hadn't even considered it. I shrugged. "My aunt and uncle came to California for the funeral, and they said I should come visit sometime, but I hadn't planned on it."

Alex looked like he was about to say something, but he didn't have time to respond because the server walked up with our food. The plastic baskets were lined with paper and I couldn't see what was inside until the guy set it in front of me. It was a huge burrito, and I smiled at the server and thanked him.

"Luisa made yours a jumbo," he said to Alex.

"Tell her thank you," Alex said. "I'm hungry."

"Ahh, you won't be hungry when you're finished with this." They both laughed and the guy turned to walk away.

"I thought mine was big," I said, with a wide-eyed stare at Alex.

He smiled. "And you have to save room for ice cream."

"Oh my goodness," I said. "I'd say there's no way, but I'm actually starving right now."

"Thank you, God, for this delicious burrito and the beautiful face I get to look at while I eat it.

Amen." Alex prayed out loud before taking a bite of his burrito.

I had to think about what he was saying because he did it with his eyes open while he stared straight at me. It sounded like a sincere prayer, so I said, "Amen," instinctually before reaching for my burrito.

I took a huge bite out of the corner and stared at Alex as I chewed. We were both gazing at each other, chewing contentedly. "So good," I said, once I swallowed my food.

Alex nodded and took another bite.

"What sports do you do?" I asked. "At the school… what kind of practices and games do you have to go to?"

"I do work with athletes from all sports… soccer, track, baseball, softball, volleyball, golf. Those are just people who make appointments and come see me. All of those teams have athletic trainers who can take care of most of their sprains and stuff. The only teams I actually work with or travel with are the football and basketball teams."

"Aren't softball and volleyball girl sports?" I asked.

"Softball is," he said. "Why?"

I shrugged as I took another bite of my burrito. We were quiet for a minute while we both chewed. "I was thinking about it as I was watching you work. About how I bet girls would fake an injury just to get an appointment with you. I would if I went to your school."

"What about if you were a landscaper? Would you still fake an injury to see me?"

I stared at him. We were chewing food and being ourselves, and yet somehow, the air between us was charged.

"If I was a landscaper, I wouldn't have to fake an injury," I said with a confident shrug. "You seem to want to take landscapers out to dinner and ice cream."

"You're right," he said. "Why would you settle for a clinical visit when I'm willing to treat you to a meal?"

Chapter 8

Alex and I went out for ice cream after we ate burritos. I ordered two scoops in a cone, and Alex ordered a milkshake. I offered to pay for the ice cream, but Alex wouldn't hear of it.

Our conversation was casual and humorous. It was a nice evening. It was warm enough to go outside, so we decided to sit at one of the tables on the patio. There was a family with two small children sitting out there with us, but there were three or four tables between us, so we didn't even look their way.

Alex and I sat there next to each other, talking and enjoying our ice cream. I ate both scoops and the cone. This was, of course, after finishing that entire burrito. The day of hard work had made me hungry, and I was so comfortable around Alex that I didn't even think twice about eating in front of him.

We sat there and talked for a while after finishing our ice cream.

"We both have to get up early for work," he said, getting to his feet reluctantly.

"I don't," I said. "But I'm cold anyway."

"I forgot you don't have anything on Tuesday."

I shivered as I stood, and Alex reached out and put his arm around me. It was the first time he had intentionally touched me all evening. I felt a rushing sensation like all of my blood suddenly left my body. Or maybe it was the feeling of all the blood returning. Either way, it made me weak in the knees. I had written about women being weak in the knees as a result of the touch of a man, but it was different when I experienced it really happening. My knees actually felt like they might give out.

I glanced downward since I couldn't contain a smile. I tried to take note of all the bodily sensations that were happening to me so that I could write about them at another time. It took me a few seconds to relax and adjust to the contact, but once I did, I leaned into Alex. He felt me respond, and he held me tighter, causing me to experience a warm, rushing sensation in my lower abdomen. It was a feeling of utter contentment.

My writer's brain did a quick analysis of what I was feeling, and one of the key sensations was that I felt protected. A huge, strong, capable man was wrapped around me, and there was a certain feeling of safety and security that somehow added to the state of happiness. I could imagine a meteor falling out of the sky, and me being safe from it with him standing over me like this.

We were quiet as we walked to his truck. I wasn't even aware that I was walking. I just sort of floated over there, having all sorts of thoughts about falling meteors and alpha males. Alex walked me to the passenger's side of his truck. We stopped in front of the door, and I was so dazed that I didn't realize he had come over there to open the door for me. I reached out for the handle. "I got it," he said, putting a hand out to stop me. His voice was deep, but his tone was soft.

He was about to open the door, step back, and let me inside.

I couldn't let him do that.

"When am I going to see you again?" I asked before he could reach for the door. I glanced at him, making eye contact. The sun had gone down, and his dark eyes seemed endless.

"When are you working at Ezekiel's again?" he asked. "Wednesday?"

I nodded and shrugged shyly. "But what about tomorrow? Would you want to hang out even though I'm not working?" I was not used to being the one asking for this type of thing. Back home, in my normal life, everyone knew who I was. Guys wanted to be with me because they liked my dad or knew I had been successful. I never found myself in a situation where a guy thought I was just a normal girl. But the thing was, I was just a normal girl, so it felt right to be treated that way.

"I get off at four tomorrow," Alex said. "Would you want to get together after that?"

"I would want that," I said, smiling.

"I think I really want that, too," he said, sounding a little surprised, and causing me to smile.

"I'm sorry if it's weird for me to ask. I just don't know how long they're going to have me working at the Tanners' farm, and I even if I'm there, I never know if I'll run into you at the stables, or where I'll be working. Dan mentioned something about an arena. I might have to be at the arena when I'm there on Wednesday. What if that happens?"

Alex scanned my face as I spoke. He made the tiniest smirk once I finished, and I squinted at him, making his smile broaden.

"You are adorable," he said. "And you don't need to explain. I want to hang out with you. Tomorrow is perfect. I'm happy you asked me."

He delivered the statements in such a straightforward way that I grinned and shook my head at him. His dark eyes were mesmerizing in the cover of darkness. His face was so big. I wanted to reach up and touch him—at least just put my hand on his shoulder or arm, his face. I had to fight against the urge to do that. I experienced a soft but almost physical pull toward him.

He stepped toward me. I thought he was going to come in for the kiss, but he reached behind me to open the truck door. He paused in mid stride with his hand on the handle. Maybe he realized that I thought I was about to be kissed and he didn't want to leave me hanging. Either way, he did not open the door. He just stood close to me, crowding my space in the most wonderful way possible and leaned down so that his face came close to my ear. I smelled the faintest mixture of masculine scents. There were traces of cologne mixed with some amazing natural male smell. He lingered there, and I did not dare move.

"I had fun with you today," he said.

"Me too."

I managed to get the words out, but I was breathless. Alex smiled because of it. He knew he had done that to me by coming so close. And just like that, he moved. In a soft but swift motion, he leaned down and kissed my cheek gently before leaning the other way to open the truck door. The kiss was sweet and thoughtful, but it was over far too quickly.

I unintentionally took a deep sighing breath as I turned to get into the truck.

"Are you okay?" he asked.

"Oh, yeah, yeah."

"Okay, good. You sighed, and I thought maybe I was out of line."

He stood in the open door even after I was settled in my seat. I smiled at him.

"No, no, it wasn't… you weren't out of line… at all. You were way in the lines."

"Okay, good. I'm really glad to know that."

We were staring at each other with serious but otherwise invisible expressions. I shook my head almost imperceptibly. Alex Holbrook was the wildcard in this whole experience. Becoming infatuated with a man was not on my list of things to do in Kentucky, and yet, it was the best thing that had happened to me in a long time. I wanted to tell him the truth of who I was, but I didn't want to lose this feeling—the feeling of someone liking me when they thought I had nothing.

He hadn't kissed me yet. It didn't seem like he was planning on doing it today. It seemed like he was too much of a gentleman. I turned to put on my seatbelt. I felt dazed. Alex went around the back of the truck to get to his door, and I just stared at nothing in particular, feeling lost in thought. I still felt the place on my cheek where he kissed me. I reached up and touched it at the memory.

I asked Alex questions about horse farming on our way back to the practice field. I didn't try to get any more information about the Tanners. I was sincerely interested in the process of breeding Thoroughbreds, and Alex knew quite a bit about it. He gave me good information and answers, but he was quick-witted and funny, and I smiled the whole time we talked. I caught myself feeling disappointed when we made it back to the practice field.

Mine was one of the only vehicles in the parking lot. It was a tough-looking SUV. I didn't even know what specific kind of vehicle it was. I squinted at the emblem, but I couldn't make it out. I was relatively sure it was Toyota. Or maybe Infinity, or Lincoln. I had no idea, actually. Courtney had taken care of talking to the rental company when she made my reservation. It was nice, and it drove a lot like my own truck at home, which was a Range Rover my father bought against my wishes for my 25th birthday. I was thankful for it and I loved it now that it was mine, but I had never been one to care about luxury vehicles. That was why I didn't even pay attention what brand my rental was.

I was staring straight at it, trying to make out the name brand as Alex drove through the parking lot. Suddenly we turned, and I realized he was going the wrong way.

"What's going on?" I asked.

"I'm just going to your car. Is that okay? Is this it?"

I realized he assumed my car was the tiny little beater hatchback that was in the middle of the parking lot, under a tree like it had been left there to die.

"Oh, no. That's not mine. That's mine over there," I said, pointing at the SUV. "That black truck thing."

"The Volvo?"

"Yes… the Volvo…" I said, making sure he was looking at the right vehicle. There were only three cars left in the parking lot… mine, the broken-down hatchback, and a gigantic dually truck that looked like you had to be eight feet tall and work on a farm to drive it.

Alex kept going, turning through empty parking spaces as he headed toward my vehicle. "This thing is brand new," he said.

"Yeah," I said, realizing that we probably should have asked for a more used vehicle to go with my backstory.

"I love it. What is it?"

"I thought you just said it was a Volvo," I said.

"It is. But I mean, what model?"

"Oh, the model… I'm not sure."

Alex pulled into the parking spot next to it, positioning me where I was closest to my vehicle. I scanned the vehicle, hoping and praying for words to be written on it that would tell me its name.

I saw XC 40 written on the back and I read it out loud. "Is that the name of it? The XC 40?" I asked.

"Yes, it is," Alex said. He stopped his truck next to mine. He put it in park but he didn't turn off the engine. He looked past me, through the passenger's window to the Volvo that was parked next to us. It was brand spanking new, and I hadn't even really considered that until this exact moment.

"That's a really nice car," he said. He was usually really jovial with me, but I could tell by the way he spoke that he was genuinely curious where I got it.

I started to formulate an on-the spot story about how I ended up with a car like that, but I just couldn't do it. I liked him too much to lie.

"It's a rental," I said. "I've only got it for two weeks. I didn't even know what kind it was until you said it."

Chapter 9

"A rental? Is your car in the shop?" Alex asked.

"No, no, nothing like that. It's a regular rental, just a rental, from a rental shop. You know, at the airport."

"Yeah, I know about rental places at the airport..." Alex said, slowly, like he was missing something.

I knew what I had to do. I had to tell him the truth. I could feel myself begin to blush as I started to speak.

"My agent rented it for me, Alex. I mean, looking at it now, I see that it's nice, but I didn't even think about that when she..." My voice was a little shaky, but I pushed past it and continued speaking. I stared at the dashboard of his truck because I could not bear to look at him. "My name is Autumn. Autumn Rains. My initials are A.J., but no one has ever called me that. Everyone calls me Autumn. That's my name. I've been telling you the truth about a lot of things while we've been talking, my whole family situation, losing my mom and everything... that's all real... but that's not all the truth. I'm a writer. I write books. Fiction fantasy books. Young adult stuff. I had a book called Evangeline's Wish that got turned into a movie."

"What do you mean, you had a book called that? You wrote it?"

"Y-yes. I wrote it."

"You wrote a book that became a movie?"

"Yes."

"In theaters? Like, a real movie?"

"Yes. I'm only here temporarily, so I rented a car. I had no idea I would meet you or hang out with you after work, or that you would see what I'm driving. I didn't even think about that. I didn't count on meeting you or spending time with you like this."

"Why are you here?" he asked, sounding a little stunned. "What are you doing at the farm? Are you even working with Dan, or did you just act like it?"

"Believe me, I worked," I said with all the conviction in the world since my back was sore from it. "I wasn't trying to fool anyone, necessarily. I just want to be unnoticed. I'm not a landscaper. I'm an author," I said. "I write books. I travel for research some. But in this case, I wanted to experience Tanner Farm as a regular person and not as an author doing research. I wanted to see what it was really like, how things really operated. I wanted to do something with the horses, but landscaping was the best my agent could do. My publisher, actually. Michael was the one who… it doesn't matter. He set it up where I was working with that landscaping place. I think the owner of it, Jesse, knows about me, but Dan and Nick and all them, they think I'm just working with them."

Alex was still staring at me thoughtfully, taking it all in. I had no idea what he was thinking.

"Why didn't you just talk to Ezekiel about it? He'd hook you up if you want to hang around the stables and talk to people. You wouldn't have to do all that landscaping."

"I don't want to tell him," I said, feeling a little panicked. I didn't plan on sharing my other secret, and I didn't want too many people to know who I was. I was sure the chances were slim that they would put things together, but I didn't know what Ben's story was or if the things my mom said were the absolute truth. I certainly had not come here to disrupt anyone's lives or cause drama.

"I don't want to tell anyone. No one but you. I'm going to stick to my plan."

"Which is what?"

"I'm just gonna go by A.J. and work with Dan and the Pleasant crew."

"So, you l-live in California, and you're just, what, here, staying in a hotel?"

"Yes," I said. "I can't even believe I'm telling you this."

"I can't believe it either," he said, being funny but wearing a serious expression.

"It doesn't change anything," I said, wanting Alex to come near me again.

"It kind of does," he said. He was wearing a smile, but it was laced with some kind of uncertainty. There was a console between us, and it was just too much—too much distance, too much separation.

"I'm telling you the truth because I like you." I said. "I'm trying to be honest with you."

"How long are you planning on staying?" he asked.

"Two weeks. This week and next."

"You just become someone else for two weeks and then disappear from here and go back to your normal life?"

"Y-yes. That was the plan, at first. But then... Alex, please just understand that I wasn't expecting to even tell you all this tonight. I wasn't prepared to hang out with you after hours, and I definitely didn't know I'd like you as a person. I know it's a shock for you to hear all this, but you have to realize, I'm trying to navigate the change in my plans, too. I felt like I didn't want to hide it from you anymore, and now it seems like I've ruined everything by telling you. I'm just hoping you'll still want to spend time with me now that you know."

"I'm still hoping you'll want to spend time with me, A—Autumn. Is that what you said your name is?"

"Yes. It's Autumn. And I very much want to spend time with you. I like you, Alex. If I didn't like you so much I definitely wouldn't be telling you this."

"Well, yeah, it'd be awesome to hang out... while you're here. I have fun with you, too." Alex was smiling and speaking sincerely, but he was acting just casual enough that my heart felt broken. I couldn't tell if he was guarded because I lied to him in the first place or if he was suddenly distant because he knew my time there was temporary.

I reached across the console and touched his arm. "I want us to act normal," I said.

"I am," he assured me with an easy smile. "I'm just thinking about everything. It's crazy that you're famous."

"I'm not that famous," I said.

"It's not like I walk around on the street and people know who I am. My dad's way more famous than I am."

"Who's your dad?" he asked.

Some voice inside of me said, "Ben Tanner," but my real voice, the words that came out of my mouth were. "Amos Rains."

"Amos is Caleb and Stella's little boy's name," Alex said. "What's your dad famous for?"

"He's a writer, too. He wrote The Sound a Soul Makes. It was popular in the nineties. It's still... I guess you never read it. Sometimes teachers make you read it in school or something."

"No, I didn't. Not that I remember, anyway. I've always been more of a math guy."

I laughed. "I cannot do math to save my life. I mean, the basic stuff, sure, but don't put a big, complicated problem in front of me. Geometry's the only non-basic one that makes any sense to me."

"Math itself makes nothing but sense," Alex said. "Concrete rules, concrete results. No style or interpretation, just right or wrong."

"Yeah, but you like style. You like art and music. You dress nice, and comb your hair just right and everything."

"I guess... but that never made me good at English. I just never became a reader. And I definitely don't want to hear other people's opinions about a book or discuss them."

"Then you just haven't found the right type of book yet."

"Maybe," he said. "Maybe I'll read yours."

"My audience is mostly women. Men enjoy them too, but you know, there's kissing and stuff."

"Men like kissing just fine," Alex said. He was serious, but he was teasing me again, and maybe even flirting, which felt wonderful.

I couldn't hold back a smile. I gave his arm a little squeeze before taking my hand off of it again. "Women definitely like kissing," I said.

"Do you have to describe it? In your books?"

"Yes. I don't have to, but I want to. I describe kissing in almost every book I've written."

"What do you say? What kinds of things do you write?"

I glanced at him shyly and he tilted his head at me, looking genuinely curious. "I don't know, I just tell how it happened naturally between two people. I just s-say what kinds of feelings and stuff they were having when it happened and how it h-happened."

I was all shaken up.

I had written my share of kissing scenes, but I never thought I'd have to talk about them at the exact moment when I wanted one to really happen. I felt like I was in The Matrix or something.

I went with it. I was out of my mind with nerves, and maybe that was what pushed me over the edge and helped me get into it. I touched his arm.

"She spoke to him in a normal tone, but her body was overrun with nerves. She touched his arm, and her hand felt like it was on fire. She glanced at him to find that he was staring back at her."

I paused and smiled, catching my breath when my eyes met Alex's. He was watching me curiously, trying to keep up with what I was saying.

"She had no idea what he was thinking," I continued. "She hoped he wasn't mad at her for keeping a secret. She hoped he would still be her friend. She wished he would kiss her."

I stopped talking for a second, waiting for him to respond.

"I'm nervous. I'd have to write it better than that," I said, unable to stand the silence. "In the book, she would say it better. He wouldn't leave her hanging."

"Are you saying I left you hanging right now?" Alex asked. "Because I have no idea what's going on. I feel like I'm in a movie or something."

I laughed. "I do too," I said. "I feel crazy. I can't believe I told you. And I certainly don't usually go around narrating my life."

"I was listening," Alex said. "Like an audiobook. I was waiting for you to say what the guy did next."

"He kissed me, of course," I said.

Alex smiled at my unrepentant response.

"He leaned over the console. He said he wasn't mad at her for saying she was a landscaper when she wasn't. And then he kissed her. He kissed her long and good."

Alex chuckled. "Would you seriously write that?"

"No. I'm sure I wouldn't seriously write half of that stuff."

His smile faded, as he scanned my face. "Would you do it, though?"

"If you're asking if I would kiss him, then, yes. A hundred percent."

"Wait, am I the him?" he asked, looking comically confused for a second.

I laughed. "Yes, you are, Alex. It's Alex and Autumn in the scene. Me and you. You and me. Autumn, me, wants Alex, you, to kiss her, me."

"You are the weirdest person I've ever met," he said with a completely straight face. I leaned in, closer to him, and he did the same, leaning toward me, both of us hovering over the console, moving slowly.

"Do you still like me even though I'm weird?"

"Yes," he said. "I'm pretty sure I like you more because of that."

We stopped moving when our mouths were right next to each other. He had soft full lips and I put mine so close to his that they touched when I spoke.

"I need to remember this," I whispered.

"Remember what?" he asked.

We were so close that I felt warm puffs of air come out of his mouth as he spoke. His mouth brushed against mine, causing a crashing wave of desire to hit me. It felt like hot liquid coursing through my body, and it took my breath away.

"This," I said, heart pounding. "I need to write something where their mouths come close like this without touching. This feeling. If I could describe the feeling. Girls would really, really like this."

"Guys would like it too," he said.

I reached up and touched the side of his face ever so delicately. This encouraged him, and he moved closer to let his lips gently touch mine. Our lips connected with the lightest touch for a few seconds before he pulled back. It happened too quickly. It was dark out and his windows were tinted. We were in a private situation, and we clearly liked each other. I stared at him from only inches away, begging without saying a word for him to kiss me again.

"It's no wonder you have a thesaurus in your purse," he said.

He was serious, and it made me laugh and shake my head.

He kissed me again, stopping me while I was in motion. He just leaned toward me and did it without hesitation. It surprised me, but I didn't jump or pull away. I went to him, meeting him, kissing him back. My hand found the side of his face again, and I gripped his jaw with my fingertips, pulling him toward me.

We kissed two, three, four times before Alex broke contact and licked his lips. His mouth parted, and he sucked on my lower lip, tugging it gently into his mouth. I let out the tiniest whimper. I didn't mean to do it. The sound just came out when I experienced the gut-wrenching wave of desire brought on by the feel of the inside of his mouth. His lips were soft and firm, and he was the most handsome, masculine, perfect man I had ever kissed—had ever laid eyes on.

I was unbelievably smitten. I had never been so enamored in my life. It was deeper than just physical attraction. In some weird way, Alex represented hope to me. That, in addition to his smart, sarcastic personality and ruggedly good looks, meant I was all-in, done-for.

Alex, ever a gentleman, did not deepen the kiss any further. He pulled my lip into his mouth, giving me a long taste of pure bliss, but he stopped at that. He pulled back, kissing me two or five or ten more times—gentle, perfect, open-mouthed pecks to the lips, over and over before finally pulling back.

"Oh goodness," I said breathlessly as he broke contact with me. "I have to remember all of this." I touched my own lips dazedly, still riding the wave of anticipation and desire. I sat back a little, taking a deep, calming breath. "Thank you for tonight," I said. I swallowed, blinking before meeting his eyes. "I'm going. I need to get back to my hotel. You have work in the morning."

Alex scanned my face. "I'm sure if we only have a limited amount of time, we should… maybe we should try to make to most of it."

"Absolutely," I agreed. "I don't know where you're going with that, but I agree already."

"We should probably try to see each other as much as possible," he said.

"We definitely should," I agreed.

Chapter 10

Alex

Ten days later

Alex Holbrook was an open and honest guy. But he currently had so many secrets that he felt like he couldn't say anything to anyone. He had to keep his amazing, unbelievable gift of land on the farm a complete secret from everyone until it was officially given to him on his birthday. And he had to keep Autumn a secret. They were two of the most surreal, wonderful things to happen to him in his whole life, and he could not tell a soul.

Okay, so maybe he did share some of it with one person.

Arthur Stuart.

This man would not repeat anything Alex told him. He wouldn't even have the opportunity to tell anyone. Arthur didn't ever see anyone who knew Alex. The two men got together every week for a standing physical therapy appointment. It was Alex's only in-home case, and it was pro bono. It all started about a year before when Alex got the full-time appointment at UK and Coach Nelson asked Alex to pay Arthur a visit as a personal favor.

Arthur had worked for many years as a janitor at the UK athletic complex. He worked into his late seventies, right up until his body simply couldn't handle janitorial work any longer. He stayed for so long because he loved the UK Wildcats. He wasn't just a basketball fan, either, he followed all sports and kept up with all the athletes. And since Alex had his finger on the pulse of the athletic program, there was no one better to visit Arthur every week and give him an update.

Alex liked the man. He had gotten to know him when he was playing basketball there. Not everyone went out of their way to be kind to janitors, but Alex had always made a point to talk to him. They developed a relationship before Arthur retired, so a year ago, when Coach Nelson asked Alex to pay Arthur a house call, Alex easily obliged.

Their meeting was under the pretense of physical therapy. Arthur had insurance that paid for some in-home care, including some physical therapy, but he preferred Alex. He said he was only able to live pain free because of Alex's help. Arthur thought that his insurance was paying Alex, but Alex wasn't in his network, and had never even filed insurance or done any sort of billing. Alex knew that Arthur's therapy was as much about the sports updates as it was about the physical therapy. Either way, he was having a positive impact on this man's life, and that was why he did it. They talked about football for the first thirty minutes while Alex guided Arthur through some stretching.

"I met a woman," Alex said, finally.

Arthur was lying on his back, and Alex was holding his leg in position, helping him do a light hamstring stretch.

"I'm sure you meet women all the time," Arthur said, chuckling and referring to Alex's youth and appearance.

"This one's different, though."

"Oh, goodness, here we go with *this one's different*. I was wondering when you'd come in here tellin' me this one's different. I thought you were smiling more than usual last week."

"Yes sir, that was when I first met her."

"Does this lady have a name?"

"Autumn." Just saying it, caused Alex's chest to swell. He took a deep breath, finishing Arthur's stretch and moving on to the other leg. "I have my heart all set on having her now, and she's leaving."

"Where's she going?"

"Back to California. She lives there. Her dad's there, and all of her friends."

He lifted Arthur's left leg, going into the same stretch on the other side.

"Maybe that's why you like her," Arthur said. "Absence makes the heart grow fonder. It's cliché, but cliché things are that way for a reason. It's because they're true."

"I'm not absent from her yet, though."

"When's she leaving?"

"Saturday," Alex said, feeling like Saturday was now his least favorite day of the week. He had never wanted a workweek to last forever, until now. It was Wednesday evening, and Alex wanted about a hundred more days before the weekend. He had managed to see Autumn every day since they met. He hadn't seen her yet today, but he had plans to meet her when he left Arthur's.

"Just relax," Alex said, shaking Arthur's leg a little.

"What's she doing in Lexington? How'd you meet her?"

"It's the craziest thing. She's an author. She writes these fantasy fiction novels. They're popular. She had one made into a movie."

"Go ahead!" Arthur said, slowly but enthusiastically. "What kind of books did you say?"

"Fantasy. There's this one where this girl goes down into a wishing well, and there's an alternate universe on the other side. That's the one that became a movie. She's got another one coming out in a couple of months."

"What's that have to do with her coming to Lexington?"

"Oh, research," Alex said. "She's working at the farm, trying to see how things run around there."

"That's pretty good. She sounds like a smart one."

"She's so smart."

"I hope she's not dragging you off to California," Arthur said. "I know a man's got to do what a man's got to do and everything, but I hope you can hold off a few more years in Lexington. At least till I'm not around anymore."

"Oh, come on, Arthur. You got about twenty good years in you." Alex stretched his leg a little farther, and Arthur moaned.

"All right, go ahead and turn over, and let's do three sets of ten of those foot raises from last week. Arthur rolled over on his bed (which was what they were using for a table). His feet were hanging off, and he began doing the small movement where he bent his leg at the knee and then let it fall straight again. One leg and then the other, slowly, over and over.

"Naw, I know I'm teasing you about staying, but are you really thinking about following her over there?" Arthur asked as he exercised.

"I don't know, honestly. We haven't talked about it yet. Both of us are just trying to forget she's leaving in a few days."

"You better start remembering," Arthur said. "If she's only got a few days."

"I know. I don't know how I'm supposed to go from seeing her every single day to never seeing her again."

Arthur let out a humorless laugh. "Sometimes that happens in life," he said.

"Well, not this time," Alex said. "But it's weird. I can't get a read. She likes me, she really does. There's no questioning the chemistry. And I know she'd be sad to leave me and pretend these two weeks never happened, but I still get the impression she's going to do it."

"What? Leave?" Arthur asked.

"Yeah. Two more on this side," Alex said, tapping Arthur's right leg.

"I thought you said you already knew she was leaving."

"I do, I just don't want it to happen," Alex said. "I'm sick over it."

"Ask her to stay. Or does she have to be California for work? Maybe she does if she's making movies."

"She's not. She writes books. Other people do the movies. I've already mentioned her staying here. I wish she would. She always says she wishes she could. Sometimes I don't know what she's thinking. I feel like I know her and trust her and love her, but there's this private side to her. She's at the farm three days a week. She was there today. I would have gone to see her on my lunch break, but she doesn't want to be herself in front of Ezekiel or Jude or the other guys at the farm. She hasn't told anyone but me that she's a writer, and she doesn't want her and I to hang out in front of them for fear that they'll catch on."

"You lost me with all that," Arthur said. "Did you say she's pretending to be someone else in front of everyone except you?"

"Yes," Alex said. "She's famous in real life, but everyone at the farm thinks she's a gardener. Dan had her pulling weeds and spreading mulch for two weeks." Alex breathed a sigh of relief, happy to have finally said those words out loud. He hadn't even told Jordan about Autumn's true identity. She knew Jordan was his best friend and had specifically reminded Alex not to mention it to him.

"Why would she want to pull weeds?" Arthur asked.

"I have no idea," Alex said, shaking his head. "How'd that feel?"

"Fine."

"Let's go ahead and stand up. We can come over here and try to step over these cones."

They went into the living room, and Arthur began slowly stepping over the cones Alex had already placed there. "No, I don't know why she's doing what she's doing. I can't quite figure this one out. She's different than other girls to begin with, but she's also more secretive than she has to be. She's friendly with people, but she's not her real self with anyone but me."

"Maybe that's a good thing."

"Maybe, in some ways, but no, I don't know, it just makes the whole thing feel more… temporary."

"Well, I've never heard you talk about a girl like this. You need to follow your heart. That's what it boils down to."

Alex didn't feel like he would leave Kentucky, but now that he thought about it, he might just follow Autumn anywhere.

"Try to get that right foot up and over the cone, not around it," Alex said, watching Arthur sidestep slowly over and along the row of cones that took up all the open space in his living room. "Take your time," he said.

"How's Tanner's foot doing?" Arthur asked.

"It's getting better," Alex said. "He's anxious to get back at it, but I'm making him take it slow. There's no sense in pushing it."

"He better listen to you. That's his second or third time on that foot."

"I know," Alex said. "And he knows that. He's smart. It's his senior year. He doesn't want to risk it."

"Cause we're counting on him."

"He knows," Alex said. "This'll be your last set."

"My hip's tight."

"Well, just take your time. This will loosen you up."

"What about Simmons? Is he gonna be ready for Saturday night?" Arthur had already asked Alex about Desmond Simmons, star running back, but it was bothering him enough that he asked again.

"I don't know yet. He's looking good, and he wants to play, but we'll see. We're judging it day-by-day. He's been on the practice field some this week, but we're taking it slow."

"I know all about that," Arthur said, taking slow deliberate steps over each cone.

"That's going to be all after this set, Mister Stuart," Alex said.

"Okay, you sure? It seemed quick today."

"Yes sir, we got it all done. You did good."

Arthur took a few minutes to finish his last set. "All right, well, you want me still doing that ball exercise this week?" he asked, looking at Alex.

"Yes sir. And the stretches. It wouldn't hurt you to do the bands for your hip."

"Oh, that's just how I'm sleeping on it funny," Arthur said.

"Suit yourself," Alex said, with a shrug.

"Thank you, Alex."

"You're welcome. I'll see you next week."

Alex picked up his cones and shook Arthur's hand before making his way to the door.

"Hey Alex," Arthur said before he stepped outside.

"Sir?"

"Don't you let her get away."

Alex smiled and shook his head. "I won't."

Chapter 11

Autumn

That same day

It was Wednesday, and I had worked at the Tanners' farm all morning. I had been working there for two weeks, and no one had caught on to who I was. No one besides Alex, of course, who I told from day one.

He knew a lot about me, and I knew a lot about him. We shared feelings and hopes and dreams. We shared childhood memories—good and bad. I was completely candid with him, telling him everything about my life. Everything except that one little fact that Ben Tanner could be my dad. I hadn't told him that because I, myself, didn't know if it was the truth or not.

I had met Jude during my time at the farm. He had dark hair and green eyes, and I took a good long stare at his face, but there was just no way to tell if he could be my half-brother or not. He was a handsome guy, and he seemed to be kind and smart like the rest of the Tanner crew. I would be happy to call a guy like Jude my brother, but there was just no way to tell.

Actually, there was. And I had gotten desperate enough to do it. DNA testing. Secret DNA testing. The opportunity had presented itself a few days ago, and I took it.

Ezekiel Tanner had hair that was about two inches long, and he wore it combed away from his face. I glanced at his back as I approached him at the kitchen sink in the stables, and I saw a strand of his hair that had come loose. No one was in the room with us, and I had no trouble reaching up and grabbing that one strand of hair, and pulling it free from the others without him noticing. I had instantly turned, grabbed my purse, and gone to the restroom. I had a compact mirror with me, and I carefully placed the hair in it.

This had happened on Monday afternoon, and I was desperate enough to call Courtney and ask for her help. I had to explain the whole paternity thing to her, but she took it better than I thought she would. She actually seemed relieved to have a more reasonable explanation for me working in landscaping. And bless her heart, Courtney came through. She had a courier come to my hotel to pick the samples up as soon as I got off work.

That was two days ago, and she told me we'd hear something by the end of the day today. I had been sitting on pins and needles waiting to hear something.

Alex had to work from 4pm to 7:30 tonight. He had to go to football practice, and then a private PT session at a patient's house. He asked me if I wanted to go with him, but I was so on edge waiting for the call about the DNA test that I told him I would catch up with him afterward. I thought I would have heard by now.

It was 7pm, and I was starting to lose hope that I would hear anything today. I had no idea whether they would contact me directly or call Courtney. All I could do was wait.

I had texted Courtney several times, and she assured me she hadn't heard anything yet. She also tried to prepare me for the worst. I could tell she thought the test might come back negative because she said they need a whole hair follicle to get a good read, or it might not have been in his hair in the first place.

I just couldn't shake the feeling that it would come back positive. My confidence only intensified when I sneezed earlier today and Ezekiel told me I sounded just like his niece.

"Oh really, I didn't know you had a niece. Is that your sister's daughter?"

"My sister does have a daughter, but you sneeze like my brother's girl, Olivia. We call her Livi. She does those baby sneezes, all in a row, like you just did."

So, yes, things had been building up, and now I was sitting in my hotel, thinking I would have heard something from the lab. It was afterhours, and I was just losing hope when my phone rang and I looked down saw that it was Courtney.

"What'd you find out?" was how I answered the phone.

"They sent it overnight express. It just got delivered to my desk. I don't know why it's so formal. I thought they would just email me.

"What's it say? Did it come back positive?"

"I didn't even open it yet," Courtney said. "The guy just left my office. I had to sign for it."

"Open it," I said. "Please."

I heard rustling.

"Before I look, let me just say one thing, Autumn, it's more likely to have a false negative than a false positive."

"What's that even mean?" I asked, unable to follow her through my nerves and excitement.

"It means that even if it's negative, there's still a chance that Ben Tanner is your dad. I mean, what if Ben and Ezekiel aren't blood brothers? What if one of them is adopted? For starters, you're trying to test Ezekiel instead of his brother, and also, you're not even sure if it was his hair. It could have been a horse hair on his shoulder.

"I saw it coming out of the bottom of his hair. It was his. It was on his collar."

"I'm just saying."

"Why? Are you looking at it? Is it negative?"

"No. I'm not looking at it. I'm trying to open it. I'm just saying, you should assume it's going to be negative."

"Why do you say that?"

There were a few seconds of silence while Courtney figured out if she wanted to answer honestly. "Because I can tell you want it to happen," she said. "I can tell your hopes are up about it, and I just want to tell you that even if it's negative, there's still a chance you're related to them. We need to get a better sample. One with Ben's spit would be amazing."

"Just can you please just see what this one says?"

Silence.

Several seconds of silence that felt more like minutes. Days. Years.

"It says the a-vun-cul-ar, whatever that means, test is one-hundred-percent certain that the hair samples provided were niece/uncle relationship. It says they have positive proof of this relationship. It says it right here."

"Are you kidding me?" I asked.

"I would not do that," she said. "I'm holding the results in my hand. It's printed on this medical paper with other information. There's this weird bar graph with lines and numbers. There's more than I can read right this second, but the big bold print in the middle of the page says that the samples provided were a match. It says it's a hundred percent. I'll scan it and email it to you."

"Oh, my gosh, oh my gosh, oh my gosh. This is crazy. I feel crazy right now. I don't even know how to feel."

I flopped back onto my hotel bed, staring at the ceiling.

"What does this mean, Autumn? Are you trying to stay there longer now?"

"No, no, no, it doesn't change anything. I just, it just… I don't know what it means. It's still just, you and I are the only two people in the world who know about it being true."

I had been telling myself that I wasn't related to the Tanners, but maybe I had been secretly hoping I was because I felt an undeniable wave of happiness as a result of the news. Maybe I was glad my mom had told me the truth, or that I was related to such a cool family. I had no idea what I was feeling. It was overwhelming. Tears rose to my eyes.

"It doesn't change anything," I said, just to fill the silence. It felt like it changed everything. "I don't think I'm going to… I don't know. I just have to think about it. But either way, Jesse knows Friday's my last day at Pleasant. It's not like I'm going to stay and work there after that."

"Yeah," Courtney said, as if that was obvious. "Okay, so, call me if you need anything else. Otherwise, I'll see you next week."

"Sounds good. Thanks again, Courtney."

"Anything for you, Autie-Boo. Enjoy the rest of your trip. Enjoy getting to know your new family."

I smiled so she could hear it in my voice, and I and told her goodbye in a regular, unaffected tone, hiding the fact that tears overflowed my eyes the second she called them my family. I hung up my phone and set it on the bed next to me. Silent tears rolled out of the corners of my eyes, down my temples and into my hair as I stared at the hotel ceiling.

I stayed there for ten or fifteen minutes before my phone rang again. It was Alex. I had been so thoroughly spaced-out from hearing that news that I didn't even realize what day or time it was. I felt surprised and happy when I saw Alex's name on my phone.

"Hey," I said. My voice was soft, but it wasn't obvious at all that I had been crying.

"Hey. You okay?" he asked.

"Yeah, yeah. I'm good. Just sitting here, being quiet. I'm tired. What are you doing?"

"I'm on my way over there."

"Yes," I said, sitting up and looking at the clock by my bedside. It was 7:30. Alex had finished with his in-home appointment, and he was coming to pick me up... as planned. "How far are you?" I asked, getting to my feet so that I could prepare myself, freshen up.

"I'm close. Maybe ten minutes by the time I park and make it up to your room."

"Okay, well, I'll leave the door open. Just come on in when you get here."

"Okay. I'll see you in a few."

We hung up, and I went straight to the bathroom. I had taken a shower after finishing my landscaping duties, but I had let my hair dry naturally earlier, and there were some touch-ups that needed to happen with a curling iron and a little powder and blush for my face. I took the next few minutes to spiffy myself up for Alex. I played pop music out of the speaker on my phone and I sang along, feeling like a nervous teenager who was about to get picked up for the prom.

I could not wait to see him. I was at the farm that day, but I didn't see him at all and felt like it had been entirely too long. I heard him give a warning knock before he walked in, and I came out of the bathroom just in time to catch him coming in the door.

Alex's stature took me by surprise every time. I smiled up at him and he smiled back. I could not stop myself from walking straight into his arms. He was wearing his work uniform—nice athletic pants with tennis shoes and a long sleeve UK athletic shirt. I buried my face into his chest, taking in the feel and smell of him. I had never dated an athlete, and it made me smile to feel his muscular body when I hugged him.

"I was missing you," he said, holding me close and kissing the top of my head.

I latched onto him tightly. "I was missing you too," I returned. "Why'd you have to work so late?" I didn't really mind that he had to work. I was just in a good mood, and I was missing him, so it was more of a way to flirt.

"I had to go to Arthur's house. He doesn't drive, and I don't have time to see people at work. I have athletes asking for me and I have to put them with someone else. Plus, he'd want to stay and talk all day. It's just better to go to his house."

"Who would he want to talk to?" I asked. "Take your shoes off and come sit with me on the couch. You can tell me all about it over here."

Alex scanned my appearance. "I thought we were going out to eat," he said. He touched his stomach. "You look like you're ready to go. And I'm hungry."

"Oh, yeah," I said. I should have been hungry, too, but I was running on emotion, and eating had been the last thing on my mind. "Yeah, we can… we can go, or we can just call room service. The restaurant downstairs is good. We could just get that and eat it up here."

"That's fine with me," Alex said. He kicked his shoes off by the door and came into the room with me.

It was a suite, and we settled in the living room, curled up on the couch. I called room service and placed an order. The TV was on in the background, but we turned it down and talked over it. I sat close to him, resting my legs over his lap. We talked about our day. One of their main starting football players was out with an injury, and we talked about him and the ramifications of him playing or not playing.

Chapter 12

It only took twenty minutes for our food to arrive, and when it did, we got out of our comfortable positions just long enough to get the food, tip the server, and get back to the couch. We ordered a lot, and we began to eat, sharing food and concentrating on eating for a couple of minutes.

"So, everybody's hoping to see Desmond Simmons on the field this weekend," I said, after a few minutes of eating. We had been talking about Desmond before room service came, so I brought it up again.

"Yeah, everybody's hoping that, for sure," Alex said. Arthur was all worried about it. I told him we were hoping he'd make a start, and he still asked me about it two or three times after that."

"That's funny. He must love football."

"He does. Basketball, too. He was asking me about Tanner's foot, and I didn't even remember telling him about it."

"Did you say he worked at UK?"

"Yeah, when I was there doing my undergrad."

"How do you go see him now? Is he still part of the program or something?"

"No, he's… I don't get paid for going there. He thinks I'm part of his in-home care, but I'm not."

"You're not?"

"No."

"Well, just tell him. I'm sure if he knew that, he'd just write you a check."

"He couldn't do that," Alex said, shaking his head a little. "He's on a fixed income. And I'm not worried about it. I see it as straight investment, anyway."

"What's that mean?"

Alex finished his bite of food before he answered. "I don't know. It's just something that clicked in my own head. About God kind of. It's hard to explain."

"Would you try?" I asked before taking a big bite of French fries.

"I don't know. It was just this one Bible verse that hit me differently one day. Miss Rhonda has them all over her house, and there's this one little sign in the living room that said something like, *greater love has no one than this, than to lay down his life for his friends*." Alex shrugged and gave me a little smile like he wasn't sure if he could explain it right. "I had heard it or seen that verse before, and I always thought of having to die. You know, like being in a position where you had to actually give your life for someone. Like a martyr. Like Jesus, or like Abraham and Isaac. And I was staring at that verse in her living room, thinking about how rare that was. And the verse just hit me in a whole new way right then. It's not my whole life that I have to give up. It's little pieces of it. Like when I go to Arthur's every Wednesday, I'm laying down my own life for him. Or when I send Mom money. It's not my whole life, all at one time, but it's still the same idea. I'm still laying down a piece of my life, and it's still qualifies as me showing the kind of love the verse was talking about. Does that make any sense?"

I nodded.

"I can see tasks, or favors, or service that way now, and it makes things more enjoyable. It makes obligations seem like... like more of an investment to me. I don't know if that makes any sense or not. I might not be saying it right."

"It does make sense," I said, dazedly, chewing slower as I thought about it.

Alex's attitude of doing tasks with joy and excellence was one of the very things that has gotten him to where he was in life, and I saw that clearly as I considered what he was saying. He was a solid rock of a man physically, emotionally, and spiritually.

Something about this conversation had me feeling compelled to tell him the truth about my relationship to the Tanners. I opened my mouth to let the words come out, but they got stuck in my throat.

Alex looked at me and smiled. "I didn't mean to preach or anything," he said. "I was just explaining why I don't mind going over there on Wednesdays."

"I wasn't thinking you preached," I said. "I actually loved what you said. I already knew you were sweet, but now I'm just overwhelmed by your sweetness..."

"I'm not too sweet," he said, speaking in a deep voice as he took a too-big, macho-sized bite of the burger. He chomped it, and it made me laugh.

"I think I might be related to Ezekiel Tanner."

My statement came out of nowhere, and Alex pulled back and stared at me like I was speaking Russian.

My heart was pounding, but I had already committed. "Ben Tanner," I said. "Ezekiel's brother."

Alex nodded.

"I think he might be my dad. My real dad, biological dad, not my real dad, but my blood dad. That's the real-real reason I came here."

"W-wait." It took Alex several seconds to get the one word to come out of his mouth. "Jude's dad is your real dad? Is that what you're saying?"

I nodded, and Alex sat up straighter on the couch, placing the tray he was holding onto the coffee table. He cleared his throat. "Are you even a writer? You must be. Your picture's all over the internet."

"Yes, I'm a writer, Alex. I've been honest with you about *everything,* but this. But it's the whole reason I came here. I wanted to meet the Tanners." I spoke slowly because I had trouble steadying my voice. "I am a writer, but I'm not here for research. I was here to try to meet some people I could be related to…" I trailed off before continuing. "That sounds weird to say that, but it's the truth."

"I'm... I can't... I'm shocked," he said, shaking his head a little. "I don't even know what to say. Your mom told you that Ben Tanner was your dad?"

I nodded. "I didn't get the message till like a week after the funeral."

"What'd your dad say?"

"Oh, gosh, no. He could never know. It would kill him. That's why the whole thing has to be a secret from everyone. That's why I can't tell the Tanners. It would just disrupt their lives, and my dad's. I'm so happy to meet them, I really am. I love knowing about them and seeing how they live, but I can't tell them the truth. For their sake and my dad's."

Alex took the tray off of my lap and set it on the coffee table next to his. I took a bite of French fries before leaving it alone. "I've had a month or so to take it in," I said, chewing. "But I know it's hard news to wrap your head around. I don't want to do that to the Tanners or to my dad."

"Well, your mom did it to you," Alex said.

"Yeah."

"And do you wish you didn't know?" he asked, being sincere.

I stared at him. I would not have traded these last two weeks for anything in the world. I stared into his dark eyes, knowing I would do it all over again, exactly the same way.

Alex started to move. I had no idea what he was doing, but he began sliding off the couch, turning toward me. He sat on the floor next to me, adjusting so he could sit comfortably while holding my legs in his arms and staring up at me.

"You have to tell them," his voice was soft, beseeching, almost a whisper.

"What?"

"Autumn, you have to tell them. Please. They would love to know that so much. They would love you so much. Jude would die if he knew you were his sister."

"Please don't tell him," I said, taking his big head into my hands. He was like a gladiator, and I smiled at how smitten I was. "Please," I said. "I'm being honest with you because I have feelings for you, and I had to tell you the truth. But with everybody else, I think it would do more harm than good. Especially with my dad."

"Please think about it," Alex said, staring up at me. "Do you think it's true?"

"I know it is," I said. "I took a piece of hair off of Ezekiel's collar, and I had it tested. DNA testing. I don't even know if he would want me doing that or if I have to have permission from him. He might be mad. Either way, the test came back positive."

"That he's your uncle?"

"Yeah, apparently. Courtney read the results to me over the phone. She said she'd email them to me. It said it was a hundred percent sure."

"Autumn, I don't even know what to say. Do you even know how excited they would be? They would have loved knowing about you being a writer, but this… this news is even better than that. Ezekiel would flip if he knew you were his niece. Please tell him. Just say you'll think about it."

"I'll think about it," I said. It wasn't a lie. I would think about it. But I wouldn't end up doing it. I knew I wouldn't tell anyone but Alex.

We talked and ate for a long while before deciding to go for a walk downtown. It felt amazing to have no more secrets. I was a hundred percent my real self with Alex now, and it was an indescribable relief. I felt happy and content, and conversation flowed naturally now that I had nothing at all to hide. We talked a lot about Ben, Jude, and Olivia. I asked him question after question. I was curious about them, and he sympathized and told me as much as he knew. I had heard enough to know that Ben wasn't as financially successful as his brother, but Alex painted a positive picture of him.

The hotel where I was staying had a nice lobby. There was a seating area with a few leather couches. It was empty and private, so we gravitated that way when we got back from our walk. We sat there and talked for another hour or so. Within that time, we got up and purchased candy bars and a drink from the hotel convenience area. I chose Rolos and a bottled water, and Alex picked a protein bar and a chocolate milk. We sat on the couch, eating our snacks and talking.

He walked me to my room once he decided to leave. He held my hand in the elevator, and once we were in the hallway, headed toward my door, he brought my hand up to his chest. He held it there, clutching me next to him. I could feel the muscular wall of his chest, and I wished he'd hold my arm there forever.

"Goodnight, Autumn," he said as we drew closer to my door.

I turned and stood on my toes, giving him a quick peck to the cheek. "Goodnight sweet Alex."

"Not too sweet," he said.

"Yes, you are," I said. "You're the sweetest thing ever."

He leaned against the wall, pulling me into his embrace. "Maybe I am," he said, giving me a cocky smile and shrug—messing with me and making me swoon.

"What time tomorrow?" I asked.

"You tell me," he said. "Think about my schedule."

"It's Thursday."

"Yep," he agreed.

"I don't have to work, and you have to work until three."

"Yes, but I'm going by the big house when I get off to take a look at Rhonda's shoulder. I'll be at my apartment by four if you want to come by and see me."

"I'd be going to the Tanner farm on my own, without Dan."

"I know," he said.

"I haven't done that before."

He gave me a nod. "I know."

"You're trying to get me to come clean with the Tanners, and I'm not. I can't."

"Think about it," he said. "They would love you so much."

"I'll think about it," I agreed, only because he was hovering over me, and he was absolutely irresistible. I stood my ground, standing tall, daring him to come closer. Alex stooped and put his face right next to mine, and I reached up, touching the side of his head, letting my fingers roam over the closely cropped hair above his ear.

"Goodnight, Autumn."

"Goodnight, Alex."

He gave me a kiss but it was the same as it always was—a glorious but light, gentlemanly kiss. Sometimes he would open his mouth just a little, but he never kissed me deeply or passionately. On one hand, I respected him for it, and on the other hand, his gentle behavior made me want to beg him to do it. I thought maybe he didn't want to kiss me like that because he knew I was leaving soon. He kissed me, five or six glorious times before putting one last goodbye kiss on my cheek.

"I'll see you tomorrow," he said. "Text me and we'll decide where."

I nodded. I wanted to ask him to kiss me again. I had nowhere near enough of his lips on mine. I stared at them, begging him to do it. He saw me staring, but he did nothing. His jaw made that little twitching motion like he was gritting his teeth.

"Sweet dreams, okay?" Alex was reluctant but determined to leave.

"Okay," I said. "Sweet dreams to you, too."

I could tell this was goodbye, so I took my room key out of my pocket and swiped it on the sensor.

Chapter 13

I regarded Alex as I slowly closed the hotel door. "Goodnight," I said, one last time as the door was closing.

"Goodnight," he said, smiling at me.

I wanted him to stop me.

I had given him time.

He could have put his foot in the door and stopped me from closing it. I gave him plenty of time to do that. I closed the door, and when I did, I turned slowly and put my back against it.

In my imagination, he was on the other side of the door with his hand in the air, getting ready to knock. I would let him in and he would kiss me passionately.

I got so excited at the thought of it that I turned toward the door and peered through the peephole. I fully anticipated seeing Alex standing there when I looked out. I was convinced he'd be there.

But there was nothing. All I could see was an empty hallway. I breathed a disappointed sigh, and then turned and rested my back against the door again. I stayed there for a minute or two, taking one last glance through the peephole before giving up.

I kicked off my shoes and went straight to the bedroom where I tossed my purse on the bed before plopping down at the foot of it. I breathed a long sigh. I could not believe I had actually told Alex. I could not believe I got a test done and it was conclusive.

I was a Tanner. I might be illegitimate, but I was a Tanner, and something about that felt a bit like royalty. It was almost as cool as being the daughter of Amos Rains. Maybe it was as cool. Maybe it was cooler. Either way, I was thankful that the man who turned out to be my biological father had some good blood—some strong stock. It gave me hope for future generations of my own family.

I still wouldn't tell my dad or Ben Tanner about it, but knowing it and being able to share it with Alex gave me a warm fuzzy feeling. I was relishing the feeling when I heard a heavy fist pound on my door. One, two, three, four times, the knocking sound came in quick succession.

I sprang off the bed and jogged that way. I took a second to glance in the peephole, but I knew it was Alex and I was whipping the door open before I could even get a good look.

He stepped inside, and I barely had time to get the door closed behind him before he lifted me into his arms. He turned with me pressing me gently against the wall while he held me there, captive between his hard body and the wall. I thought he might say something to explain why he was back, but there was none of that.

Alex kissed me like he had never kissed me before. He didn't say a word. He just let his mouth fall on mine. I stretched up to give him better access.

Alex used the wall as leverage, pinning me, holding me, kissing me like he was no longer patient. I opened my mouth to him and let him set the tone and the rhythm. He covered my mouth with his, adjusting me, turning and moving slowly to get better angles. It was only a kiss, but it felt like more than that. It felt like more was happening between us. This kiss connected us physically in a way we hadn't connected yet. He was possessive and greedy, and it felt so good that I experienced an elevated type of physical pleasure. I didn't know a kiss could make a person feel like this. I gave over to the sensation, holding him tightly and letting him guide our movements.

I had been seeing him every day for two weeks. We had kissed and held hands and we both seemed to like each other, but never had he ever handled me this way. I actually wasn't sure that any man in my life had ever kissed me like this. Alex was amazing. He was deliberate and passionate, and he guided me and held me. And he tasted good. His mouth was warm and soft and slick and it tasted like the faintest hint of chocolate. Alex stood over me like a giant mountain, and I felt like I never wanted to be apart from him. He slowed down and kissed me gently before deepening it again. This happened three or four times, and I always welcomed it when he kissed me deeper.

He held me there, kissing me for what must have been five or ten minutes before he finally pulled back. "Okay," he said. "Sorry. I got downstairs and was headed to get my truck, and I… just couldn't leave. I just had to come back up here for a minute."

I stared at him, searching his impossibly dark eyes. "Thank goodness you did," I whispered slowly. I felt so passionate and fervent when I said it that it caused tears to spring to my eyes. I felt them begin to water. I blinked.

"Are you crying?" he asked.

"I'm just happy," I said, stretching up to kiss his cheek. "I'm so happy you came back. I was wishing you would."

"Good," he whispered, smiling at me.

I nodded. "It is good."

"I like you, Autumn," he said.

"I like you too." I said. I touched the side of his face when I said it, and I thought that *I loved him* and didn't just like him.

"Goodnight, beautiful,"

"Goodnight Alex. The boy who makes my heart race."

"I'll see you tomorrow," he said with one last kiss on my mouth. His lips stuck to mine, and we both smiled when he pulled back.

"I'll see you tomorrow," I agreed, feeling utterly spent.

In those seconds before Alex walked out, I wanted to do something crazy like ask him to marry me. I had never met someone so good and honest and stable. I wanted to beg him to run off to Vegas with me that night. I thought maybe we could just go to the justice of the peace right here in Lexington tomorrow. I was swept away with love and attraction. I was so dazed in this moment of kiss-induced bliss that I almost seriously proposed. It seemed totally logical at the moment. But I didn't. I kept my mouth closed, taking it all in, trying to remember every sight, sound, and feeling of this moment.

Alex kissed the back of my hand and moaned as he reluctantly tore himself away from me. We said goodnight to each other a second time, and this time, I smiled and drifted to my bedroom, knowing he wasn't coming back. He was gone for the night.

I fell asleep smiling.

***

I found out that it was an actual thing that time flies when you're having fun. Because just like that, I found myself packing for the trip home.

It was currently 6am on Saturday.

I had to be at the airport at 7:30, and Alex was on his way to pick me up so that we could eat breakfast on our way. We had already taken care of my rental vehicle. He took me to turn it in the night before and then he gave me a ride back to my hotel, knowing that he would pick me up in the morning.

He knocked on my door at six-on-the-dot. He was wearing jeans and a t-shirt with a light hoodie.

"Good morning. Is it cold?" I asked, reaching up to touch his collar. He leaned down to kiss my cheek, and I got a whiff of his cologne. It could have been shower gel because it wasn't strong, but it was a clean masculine scent that I associated with Alex now.

"I wish I could have this shirt," I said, tugging at his t-shirt. "To take with me."

Alex looked down at it casually as if he didn't even remember what shirt he had on. "You can have it," he said. "I'll take it off right now."

"No, we're going to breakfast," I said. I reached out and put my hand on his chest. I was pretending to stop him from taking off his shirt, but really, I just wanted the excuse to touch his chest. "I do want it, but just leave it on for now and take it off at the airport."

He stared down at me, scanning my face. "Don't leave," he said.

"I know. My heart hurts."

"Then don't go," he said. "Just stay and we'll figure it out."

I breathed a sigh. "I have to go. I have to get started on publicity for my new release, and I have to start wrapping my head around the next one. Plus, one of my friends was getting married, and there's this engagement party next weekend. I'm supposed to go to Sedona for that."

"I understand," he said. "I have work stuff, too."

"I know. You'll have to call and let me know how the game goes tonight. How Desmond does."

"He'll do fine."

"Still, you can call and tell me."

"Okay," Alex said. He smiled a little, but there was an edge of regret to his expression. "You're so beautiful," he said.

I smiled at him. "And you thought that even when I was a landscaper."

"Yes, I did. I wanted you the minute you started shoveling pasta into your mouth." He laughed, and I made an overly-defensive face as I fake-pounded his chest.

I grinned at him, blinking and biting shyly at my bottom lip. "I'm gonna come back and see you. This isn't goodbye forever, I promise. I just need to think about things and sort things out."

"I know it's a lot to go from having almost no family to meeting the Tanners. I can't imagine finding out you're related to a whole big group of people like that. But I also can't imagine a better family if it was going to happen to you."

I touched the side of his face. "I'll just go and take a little while to think about things. But I'm telling you right now, I don't think I'm going to like being apart from you. I'm dreading it. I didn't expect this, Alex." It made my heart race to be so vulnerable with him.

"I didn't expect it, either. Go do some thinking or whatever you need to do. But just tell me I'll see you again."

"You'll see me again. I'll come back here."

"Okay," he said. "That's all I need."

Chapter 14

Alex

Three weeks later

It was a big weekend at the Tanner household.

Jordan had just started training camp, but he, Mica, and their eight-month-old son made the trip home for the weekend since there was so much going on. Alex's birthday fell on a Thursday, and the family was planning a simple birthday dinner celebration for that. And then that Saturday, the Tanners were hosting the annual UK basketball banquet.

They had a lot going on. That was why Alex was confused to see Ezekiel on campus with a tray of food and some balloons that Thursday at noon. Sure, it was his birthday, but Ezekiel had never shown up at the college with balloons.

"You didn't have to do all this," Alex said, meeting him in the hallway.

"I didn't do it," Ezekiel said, as they turned and headed toward the training room. "I've got it," he added when Alex tried to take the package from him. "I'm just the messenger. These are cookies from

Allison's bakery. She figured you'd want to share with everyone."

"Who, Miss Rhonda? Or Allison?"

"Oh no, these are from Autumn."

Alex couldn't think straight for a second. He had no idea Autumn had talked to Ezekiel. He had no idea Ezekiel knew her real name was Autumn.

"Are you okay?" Ezekiel asked, seeing Alex's stunned expression.

"I'm, yes, I'm just surprised to… did you… when did you talk to Autumn?"

"We started talking a few days ago. She got a hold of Rhonda through email and told her everything about coming here undercover."

"Everything?" Alex asked, looking directly at Ezekiel as they walked.

"About her being a writer," Ezekiel said. "Rhonda already knew about her books. She knew just who Autumn was. And we've all read that one her dad wrote. Isn't that crazy that her dad is Amos Rains? I thought that book was from the twenties or something."

"Yes," Alex said, feeling speechless. He had talked to Autumn as recently as yesterday, and he had no idea she had been in touch with Ezekiel and Rhonda. He wondered why she hadn't told him.

Ezekiel and Alex stepped into a kitchen area that was used mainly for the coaches. Ezekiel set down the tray, nodding and acknowledging another man who was sitting at a table near the wall.

"We'll leave this here, and you can follow me outside for a minute." Ezekiel said as he started to make his way toward the door.

"Okay, but what's going on? Is Autumn here?"

"No, no, nothing like that. I don't want you to get your hopes up. I promise, it's nothing like that. It's just a gift. You have a little birthday gift outside."

Alex followed Ezekiel even though he was confused.

"Apparently, Autumn is fond of you, Alex. Because she called and told us all that about being a writer. She said she was just planning on working on the farm for a while, sneaking in and sneaking out. But she didn't plan on meeting you."

"She said that?"

"Yes," Ezekiel said. "And then she asked me to choose between three of these and decide which one you would like best for your birthday. Of course, we had to get Jordan in on it."

"Three of what?" Alex asked.

They were walking out of the glass doors as they spoke. Ezekiel hesitated just long enough to stop and pull something out of his pocket. He handed a small black object to Alex. Alex turned it over in his hand, but he knew what it was just from the size and shape and the fact that a keychain was attached to it.

"What is this?" he asked.

Ezekiel pointed to the parking lot, and Alex looked up to find Jordan standing in the back of a brand new pick-up truck. Jordan hit the top of it like a wild man, and let out a yell of excitement before waving Alex over.

Alex glanced at Ezekiel. "Whose truck is that?"

"It's yours," Ezekiel said. "Autumn bought it for you. She had us pick the one we thought you wanted, but she bought it. We had nothing to do with that. All we had to do was pick it out and pick it up."

"Come here, son!" Jordan yelled excitedly from the parking lot.

Alex jogged over to the truck.

"This thing is baaaaad," Jordan said. "It's like the one Eric just got. It's got a system, too. You gotta crank it when you get in."

Alex approached the truck, staring at it, feeling like he was in a dream. Jordan jumped out of the back, hugging Alex to congratulate him.

The truck was gorgeous. It was a flat gray color with little red details here and there. It was decked out with tinted windows and jacked-up tires, and every available option. It was bigger than his current truck, but it wasn't huge. It was perfect, honestly. He couldn't have picked a better one himself. Alex was astounded. He couldn't believe this was happening. But there was tons of back-patting by Jordan, and that kind of excitement would only be happening if this was real.

"Woo-hoo, son, look at this whip, whip, let her rip! When'd you get so close to this writer woman? What's she doing buying you a truck for your birthday? Why didn't you tell us about her?"

"She was… she didn't… she was pretending to do landscaping when she was here. No one knew who she was, and y'all didn't even know we were seeing each other, so I just…" Alex trailed off as he climbed into the driver's seat.

"It's nice, huh?" Jordan said, watching Alex stare at the interior.

"She can't do this," Alex said.

"She already did," Jordan said. "Her bank was ready. She just asked us to pick the one you'd like and deliver it to you at work. Honestly, you would have loved any of the three she picked. We almost went for the Toyota. It was just as nice as this one."

"She wrote you a note," Ezekiel said. "It's in the other seat."

Alex looked down at the seat, the gorgeous black and grey leather seat. He noticed an envelope with his name on it. He reached for it and then brought it to his lap but didn't open it.

"It drives nice," Ezekiel said. "I drove it over here and Jordan followed me."

"I was about to drive it, but the little kid wanted to," Jordan said, referring to his dad.

Ezekiel shrugged. "You got to pick it out," Ezekiel said. "I wanted to see if you made the best choice for Alex."

"I can't even believe this. I feel like I'm dreaming right now."

"Well you're going to have to dream that you drive it over to the house tonight for your birthday dinner. Miss Rhonda was upset that she didn't get to go with us to pick it up. She had to do a volunteer thing this morning."

"Tell her I'll drive it over tonight," Alex said.

He hopped out of the truck, closing the door, and shaking his head at how unbelievable the whole moment was.

"Autumn sent the cookies and balloons, too." Ezekiel said. He patted Alex's shoulder.

"I think she likes him," Jordan said.

"You think so?" Ezekiel asked, teasing Alex.

"I've never had a menu of three trucks to choose for a friend," Jordan said. "And the day's not over yet." Jordan reached in and tried to pinch Alex as he walked by. Alex defended and the two of them locked arms, Jordan trying to pinch him and Alex blocking it.

"What's on the menu tonight?" Jordan asked, as they broke apart. Jordan and Ezekiel started walking toward Jordan's truck, but he looked back, waiting for Alex's answer.

"I think pizza," Alex said.

"Don't forget to drive this over so my wife can see."

"I will," Alex said.

He waved at Jordan and Ezekiel with his left hand, which was his empty one. The envelope from Autumn, along with the keys to the truck were clutched in his right. Alex had a small office, and he went straight to it and sat down at his desk so that he could open the note. He started reading it right away.

Happy Birthday to my sweet Alex! I miss you and I wish I could be there with you! I know you were not expecting a vehicle for your birthday. I know you would not let me buy this if I had asked your permission. Please understand that I have the money to purchase this, and it makes me feel amazing to do it. It will give me enjoyment to think about you driving it and having fun with it. I knew it would raise questions with the Tanners, so I went ahead and told them the truth about my occupation. They know that I live in California and that you and I hit it off when I was at the farm doing research. They were so happy to help me pick it out for you, and it made my heart happy to see how much they loved you and looked forward to making you happy. I hope they picked a good one. They assured me you would love it. I love you and I hope you have the best birthday ever!
Sincerely,
Autumn

They had never said I love you before, and there it was, at the end of the third-party-printed note for all the world to see. I love you. She bought him a truck, for goodness sake. She must love him. She had told the Tanners who she was. (Mostly.) That had to mean something. She wouldn't have done that if she didn't want to be a part of his life.

He read the note again. He was in the middle of reading it for the second time when Coach Jones stuck his head around the corner. "Are those cookies in the lounge up for grabs?"

"Yeah, man, get whatever you want outta there."

"All right, cool, I'll grab one. Happy Birthday."

"Thanks."

Alex worked for a few more hours. Everyone saw the cookies and balloons and they wished him happy birthday because of it. But no one knew there was a brand new truck in the parking lot. Alex knew it, though. He looked out the window what must've been ten times just to make sure that it was still sitting there.

He was amazed as he drove it to the farm after work. It was difficult not to be in straight denial that it belonged to him. He had a couple of hours to spare before getting together for pizza with the Tanners, and the first thing he did when he got back to his apartment was call Autumn.

She picked up on the second ring. It sounded like she was driving.

"Hello birthday boy," she said. "Should I sing to you?"

"Please sing," Alex said. "Just because I want to hear you."

"Courtney's right here in the car with me, or I would," she said. "But happy birthday. Are you having a good day?"

He could hear her smiling, and he imagined what it looked like. "Yeah, I am," he said. "I can't believe what you did."

"You like it?"

"Yes. It's amazing. I want to Facetime you later so you can see it. What are you and Courtney doing?" he asked.

"She's, uh, taking me to a signing. A book signing. It's an underground thing at this tiny bookstore. She gave clues about it that only super fans would put together. We're only expecting like ten or fifteen people."

"That sounds fun," Alex said.

"I know, it is. But enough about me. How's your day, birthday boy?"

"You bought me a truck, and you told me you love me in that note."

He said the words so matter of fact that Autumn paused for a few seconds.

"I d-did," she said, stuttering. "And I do. Courtney's right here though. What'd you think about the truck? Did Jordan do okay?"

"I love it so much," he said. "And I love you, too, Autumn. I'm happy you wrote me that."

"I'm happy too," she said, trying to sound natural. "I'll call you later when we're done with this signing."

"We'll be eating dinner, but I'll have my phone on me, so just call when you can."

"I will," she said. "Happy birthday."

"Thank you," he said. "Thank you so much for this. It's awesome."

"Take a picture for me, please."

"I will. I'll text you."

"Okay, good. Talk to you soon."

Chapter 15

Autumn

I found, as the days and weeks passed, that I could not live without Alex Holbrook.

I clung to that t-shirt and the remnants of his smell that lingered on it. I didn't know what would change and exactly how things would play out, but I had to be near him. A t-shirt and some vivid memories would no longer do the trick. I could no longer stand the distance.

He was celebrating a birthday, and I knew it would be the perfect time to surprise him. I had been in touch with the Tanners. I told them who I was, professionally, and they helped me purchase a truck as a birthday present.

They did not know I was going to Lexington to surprise Alex, though. That was how much I wanted it to be a surprise. I didn't tell a soul that I was going to Lexington.

I bought a one-way ticket and arrived on his birthday. My plan for the immediate future was to work from the hotel room while Alex was working, and otherwise spend every waking hour with him.

I made a reservation in the same hotel where I had stayed before. I was planning on staying for at least a couple of weeks. I had no plan, honestly.

I had been in touch with the Tanners about the vehicle, so I had their phone numbers. I would call one of them that evening before Alex was scheduled to arrive at their house and tell them that I was in town.

I knew it was a slight gamble. There was always a slim chance that surprising someone cold like that could end up in disaster. Like what if I showed up at the party and Alex's other girlfriend was there? I knew that wasn't going to happen, though. I knew Alex was fond of me and that there would be none of that type of disaster. And I also knew that keeping the Tanners in the dark about my trip would be my only chance at not having the surprise ruined.

Alex called me when I was at the airport. I picked up because he knew I would. I hadn't talked to him yet and it was his birthday. I told him I was with Courtney when he called.

I had dreamed about doing this underground book signing where I gave clues and a few of my top fans showed up and we hung out and ate cheese and crackers and caramel apples. I told Alex that's what I was doing even though I was being driven through the parking lot at the Lexington airport.

I only had about an hour to spare at my hotel before I had to make arrangements to go to the Tanners', so I knew I needed to talk to Alex when he called, and I knew I needed to act natural. We talked about his truck. He was so shocked from it that it was easy to have a conversation without him putting any pieces together about my whereabouts.

We hung up, and the next hour was a rushed whirlwind where I checked into my hotel, freshened up, called Rhonda Tanner, and planned to head to their house. I told her that I would be at her house in thirty minutes.

She had no idea about the extent of my and Alex's relationship. All she knew was what I had told them. I gave her the news that I was already in town and that I had plans to come over, and she handled it as kindly as could be expected. She was surprised, but she rolled with it and told me to, "Come on over, sweetheart." She told me that she wasn't sure if Alex would be there or not by the time I arrived, but that she would text and let me know.

My driver was late. He had gotten into a fender bender (not his fault) after he gave me a ride from the airport. Everyone was fine, but it was a small company, and it took him some time to get that squared away and get his hands on a different vehicle. I thought it would happen faster than it did. I sat in my room and waited for his call.

Finally, I met him downstairs and gave him the address to the Tanners' house. Rhonda sent me a text right when we got on the road.

Rhonda Tanner:
Hey, Alex is here. Just wanted to let you know. Several others, too.

I texted her back instantly.

Me:
Sorry. My driver was late, but I'm on my way now. The GPS says fifteen minutes.

Rhonda Tanner:
As of now, we're all in the blue living room, the back one, closest to the kitchen. I'll leave the front door open, and you can come in and follow our voices. Is that a good plan? Or do you want to knock?

A rush of excitement hit me as I considered the options. In all of my daydreams about it, I had always walked in. Never did I imagine myself knocking.
I texted her back.

Me:
I'll just walk in, if that's okay.

Rhonda:
Sounds perfect. Just come in the front door and walk through the house and toward the right. We're just getting ready to eat. I could stop them, but that might tip him off.

Me:

No, don't stop them. You guys eat. Thank you for the update.

Rhonda:
He'll be so excited. He's already been in there talking about you.

Me:
Awesome, I'm happy! Thank you, and see you in a few.

I was carrying a small handbag, but I was otherwise emptyhanded as I got out of the car. My payment and tip were already squared away with the driver, so I just thanked him and told him goodnight. I knew I wouldn't need a ride back to the hotel since I'd be with Alex.

I thought about little things like future rides back to my hotel as a means to calm my nerves as I walked toward the house. Their front entryway was gorgeous with stone and wood and a huge double door with windows. I reached out and opened the door carefully.

I tried to look natural and not too sneaky just in case someone was standing on the other side, watching me. I stepped inside. The entry way was empty. It was huge and open with gorgeous marble floors.

I didn't waste any time looking around for them. I began making my way into the house, veering to the right since Rhonda had mentioned that. I walked through a gigantic open area with windows on the right. I had on soft-soled leather flats, and I made my way through the giant open space with virtually no sound. *Tap, tap, tap, tap, tap...* I gently jogged across the space. And then I remembered that I should slow down since I was already breathless for other reasons. I walked the rest of the way. I couldn't see anyone, but I heard the talking getting louder, so I knew I was getting close. It sounded like a lot of voices.

Then one came out louder than the rest. "Seriously, though, Alex. I'm so happy you'll be building a house out here. I'm pumped about having you close."

I stopped walking when I heard that statement. It seemed heartfelt, and I waited so that I didn't walk in during a touching or private moment.

"I'm pumped, too," I heard another man's voice say.

"I'm just… speechless," Alex said. "I don't even know what to say."

"Say you'll leave those trees on the lot," a guy said.

"Yeah, there are some nice oaks on that lot," Ezekiel said. "At least three that I can think of."

"Happy birthday!" a woman's voice said in a cheery tone.

"Thank you guys from the bottom of my heart," Alex said. "I seriously love you."

A few people answered with their version of "We love you," and then multiple conversations began happening at once. It sounded like people were talking while eating. It was as good a time as any for me to walk around the corner and reveal myself, but I found that it was almost impossible to make myself move.

I had to concentrate hard to be able to take that first step. One foot in front of the other for three, four steps before I could see any of them. I had to really push myself to go around that corner.

The family was gathered in a cozy living room. The furniture was white, but the walls and accents were jewel tones of jades and blues. There were big couches and chairs, and in the center was a circular sunken down area. It looked like they were all sitting on the floor around a giant circular coffee table. There were ten or twelve people sitting around with pizza and drinks. It was a family style meal if I had ever seen one.

Rhonda noticed me first. She had been looking out for me so she made eye contact as soon as I stepped into sight. I saw her smile and widen her eyes at me, and two people turned my way when they saw her do that. They were far enough away that I had to take a second to scan faces and find Alex.

It all happened so fast after that. Alex glanced my way, and the next thing I knew, he sprang to his feet and began moving in my direction. He broke into an instant run, leaping and hopping, and making his way to me using the quickest possible route. Alex jumped over an entire couch, front to back. It was an oversized piece of furniture, and he sprang over it like it was nothing, causing everyone in the room to cheer.

I expected him to embrace me. I knew he was going to do it. I could tell he was going to take me into his arms the minute he came close enough. He was huge and he was headed for me like a freight train. I giggled and braced myself at how quickly he was moving.

Alex did not stop when he reached me. He bent down and took me into his arms, tossing me over his shoulder and hauling me out of the room. It took me so by surprise that I let out a squeal. I thought I could hear protesting from the other side of the room, but really, all I could hear was bumping and breathing, and the shifting of fabric as Alex carted me away.

Chapter 16

Alex stopped and set me down once we made our way around the corner and out of sight of everyone else. It was the open room where I had just been, but Alex positioned us near the wall. He handled me carefully, but he moved with speed and determination.

After he set me down, he pulled back just enough to focus on me. He took a few seconds to stare into my eyes, tilting his head and looking expressive and curious, asking me a hundred questions without saying a word.

I just stayed quiet, looking back at him. I would have agreed to anything he asked me right then.

Alex pulled me in, wrapping his arms all the way around me, moving, taking me into his embrace and fitting my body against his as snuggly as possible. I hugged him back, wrapping my arms around his big tree-trunk waist and staring up at him.

"You left everyone back there," I said, smiling up at him.

"They'll live." He leaned down and kissed me. He looked me straight in the eyes as he pulled back. "When did the... how did you... when did you get here? How are you here? How long are you staying?"

"I flew in an airplane," I said, choosing one of his questions to answer first. "And I don't know yet."

"You don't know, what, yet?" he asked. "What does that mean?"

"I don't know how long I'm here. I think a week or two, at least."

"When's your return flight?"

"I didn't get one yet."

Alex made sudden movements when I said that. He gripped onto me tightly, and lifted me off my feet. Bowing his chest and squeezing me tightly. His feet didn't leave the floor, but he stretched out, turning into a rocket ship that was blasting off. He was gentle with me, but I might as well have been a doll strapped to an actual rocket with our size and strength difference.

I giggled quietly at his explosive excitement. Alex kissed me as he set me to my feet. Or maybe it was me who kissed him. Either way, our mouths came together. Passion and relief flowed instantly through us. I missed him so much. I had almost forgotten what it felt like to kiss him. We kissed each other deeply, in several rhythmic movements where we connected fast and hard. Alex broke the kiss way too fast. I felt dazed when he pulled away.

"Shhhhh," he whispered in my ear.

I heard voices and footsteps for a second or two, and I barely had time to wipe my mouth and take step backward before I saw people come around the corner.

"See, I told you!" Rhonda pulled on Jordan's arm, trying to get him to turn around and go back the other way.

"I thought you ran out on your own party," Jordan said. "I didn't even get to meet Autumn before you drug her outta there."

Jordan reached in to hug me. He was an inch or two shorter than Alex, but he was still a big guy, and I smiled and hugged him back. I was glad people in Kentucky were accustomed to hugging because it felt nice. I imagined he knew he was my cousin even though I knew he didn't.

"I'm Jordan."

"Autumn," I said. "I missed you when I was here before."

"Yeah, Dad said he got to meet you a few times. But he didn't know… it was a surprise to all of us when you called and said for us to choose a truck. I mean, a flavor of cake, or color of tie, I could see… but a *truck*? That was a new one for us."

Jordan was laughing and teasing me, but the way he talked to me made me feel so welcome and loved. We started walking back to the table with them. Alex reached out for my hand as we walked, and I gladly went to him. I was nervous about getting caught at the end of a passionate kiss and about meeting and encountering all of these people, but I did my best to shake it off.

We all rounded the corner together, talking as we made our way to the table. But I was in la-la land. *How had I even gotten myself into this?* Love could make a person get herself into the oddest situations.

Everyone was indeed sitting on the floor. The coffee table in the living room was set up that way. It was a beautiful round table situated on a tile floor. There were spill-proof pillows and cushions everywhere. It obviously wasn't the first time this family had gathered around that table.

I knew everybody wasn't present, but it still seemed like a lot of people. Most of them stood up when we approached the table. A couple of the mothers were tending to babies, and they just sort of smiled and waved at me from where they were sitting. I shook hands and bowed in greeting as Alex went around the table, introducing me.

"You just met Jordan. This is his wife, Mica, and their little boy. Wolfgang. Wolfie."

"We all call him Wolfie," Ezekiel said.

"This is Ezekiel and Rhonda. You know them, I think. Here's Jude, and his wife, Andy. That's their little baby in the seat. How old?" Alex asked, looking at Jude.

"Three months," Jude said.

"Benjamin," Alex said. He glanced at me.

"I love babies," I said, talking to Jude, but also sort of everyone. I did love babies, and there were plenty of them around, so I figured it was a good thing to say.

"You can hold little Benny and the jets when he gets up," Jude said when he heard my comment.

I smiled at him, and our eyes met. I felt a bit like I wanted to cry. It wasn't the first time I met him, but it was the first time I'd seen him since I knew for sure that we had the same dad. Thankfully, Alex kept right on introducing me to everyone else at the table.

"This is Zeke and Allison. They have twins. These two," Alex said, pointing at two different toddlers. "Ezekiel the third, we call him Big E or Easy E. And his twin sister, the princess, Juliette."

"Justin and his crew are coming, too," Rhonda said. "But we'll tell you their names when they get here."

"It's nice to meet all of you," I said, waving at everyone as we took our places at the table.

"I read your book," Mica said. "Evangeline's Wish. I saw the movie too. We were just talking about you after Alex drug you off, and I told them I saw that movie the day it came out."

"I saw it, too," Allison said.

"What movie are y'all talking about?" Andy asked.

"Autumn's an author," Mica said. "We were talking about it just now. You were tending to Ben, but that's what we were saying when Alex got up and ran off. Autumn was here doing research for a book and that's how she and Alex met."

"She was working with the landscaping place," Ezekiel said. "Really getting into character."

I chuckled as I sat down.

Alex drew me near. He wasn't overboard about it, but he definitely touched me and kept me close.

I felt like part of the gang with how they treated me, though. They were natural and sincere around me… like I was welcomed into the fold. They knew I was a writer, and they asked me a little about it, but it seemed like they were more concerned with the fact that I cared for Alex.

I did care for Alex.

Some part of my soul loved to find that my secret family was actually quite wonderful. But far and away the best thing to come out of the whole situation was Alex Holbrook. *Who knew my way in would be through an outsider? Who knew I'd find myself falling in love?* This family loved him, too, that was obvious. He was one of them. They all acted like they were brothers. They talked and smacktalked and teased each other constantly. They were all handsome and confident and competitive, and their banter was constant and funny.

Justin and Lindsay came in with their seven-year-old daughter and toddler son. They introduced themselves to me and instantly went for a place at the table, squeezing in where they could and helping themselves to pizza.

"I knew we were gonna have Jet's Pizza for Alex's birthday," Justin said.

"Cheap date," Ezekiel said.

"Jet's pizza's the best!" Justin said, taking a big bite out of a slice.

"Yeah, Justin drove about ninety down New Circle to get here," Lindsay said.

Everyone laughed when she said that, and she looked at Alex. "Happy birthday," she said.

"Thank you," he answered with a nod. "I know people say this about every birthday, but this seriously is the best birthday ever."

"He means it this time," Jordan agreed. "Your boy got two acres at the edge of Big Woods Lane and a new truck."

"What?" Justin said, taking another bite of pizza.

"You heard him right," Alex said. "I'm still trying to process it."

"Two acres on the farm?" Lindsay asked. "For real?"

"It's that little piece of woods out on the back road by Jude's," Ezekiel said.

"Oh, where the blackberries are?" Justin asked.

"Yeah," Ezekiel said. "It's shaped a little funny, but..."

"But aren't we all?" Rhonda said, finishing her husband's sentence.

"Oh, good. That's a good piece of land for you over there, Alex," Justin said. "You should build a modern looking house in all those woods. I could see Alex doing something weird like that. Something with a bunch of windows and an elevator."

"How about an escalator?" Ezekiel suggested.

"Or a spiral staircase," Mica said.

I was about to agree with her about the spiral staircase idea when Jordan spoke. "Yeah, I'll give him the number of that architect I used. He does all the contracting."

"What's this about a truck?" Justin asked.

"Alex's lady bought it for him," Jordan said. "She writes books. Like big time. The ones that get made into movies."

"One did," I said. "And hopefully this next one."

Justin stared at me stiffly and began talking slowly like he was wary. "So, you're saying your new… girlfriend… who's also… famous… bought you a truck… for your birthday?" He was being so overly dramatic with the delivery that everyone laughed.

"Y-yes," Alex said.

We were sitting next to each other. It sounded like he wanted to say something more, but he settled for simply agreeing. He put his hand on my leg, and I leaned into him.

"She sent Jordan and E to my work this morning with a new truck, and then she just walked in the door a few minutes ago. I had no idea she was coming. I thought she was in California until like twenty minutes ago. She just walked in and stood over there."

"Alex jumped over three different pieces of furniture getting to her," Rhonda said. "I thought he was going to break his neck."

"Yeah, and then he tackled her and ran off with her. We thought he left. We just sat here for like three minutes, wondering who that was and what just happened."

"We knew who it was," Rhonda said. "She called just a few minutes before she came over."

"I only just arrived in town this afternoon," I clarified. "And I wanted to surprise him."

"You're so smart not to tell my parents," Zeke said. "They cannot hold a secret to save their life."

"Hey!" Ezekiel said, defensively.

"Dad can keep a secret. It's Mom," Jordan said.

"Hey, I kept it from Alex that Autumn was on her way, didn't I?"

"She did keep it a secret," Alex said. "I had no idea."

"What book did you write?" Lindsay asked, looking at me.

"Evangeline's Wish."

"Oh, gosh, seriously? You're Autumn Rains? I loved that book! I can't wait for Magnolia Borderlands. I already preordered it."

"Oh, thank you. I could get you a copy… if I would have known."

"Oh, no, I already ordered it. But I'll have to get you to sign it sometime." Lindsay laughed, looking dumfounded as she bit into a slice of pizza. "Alex sitting over there, holding hands with Autumn Rains," she said, shaking her head absentmindedly. "You never know what will happen to you in a day."

Chapter 17

"I'm going to get Ben's diaper bag out of the truck," Jude said a few minutes later, while Justin and his family were still eating.

"Wait, we haven't sung to Alex," Rhonda said, seeing him stand up but not realizing what he had said.

"I'm just running to the truck for a second," Jude said. "Does anybody need anything from the kitchen?"

"Probably a couple more of those juice pouch things," Rhonda said.

"I parked right next to you," Alex said. He took out his keys and tossed them to Jude. "You should let Autumn follow you out there so she can check out the truck she bought before the sun goes down."

"Oh, no, that's okay," I said. "He's just running out there for something else."

"I want to check it out, too," Jude said. "Come on, Autumn. Walk out there with me. Have you not seen it?"

"I was looking at it coming in," Justin said. "It's nice. I thought Uncle E got a new truck."

"You coming?" Jude asked, looking straight at me.

I knew what Alex was doing. He wanted me to walk out there with Jude. The thing was, I liked Jude. I was proud that he was my half-brother. I had laughed at his jokes. I had been too obvious, and Alex had spurred me on because of it.

I followed Jude through the kitchen.

"How is it being a new dad?" I asked him.

"It's amazing," he said. "That little boy… it's crazy how something can just steal your heart like that. I just look at him, and I see that he's a piece of me, you know. My blood."

He was being sweet and sentimental about his son, but I just kept thinking about it applying to Jude and me. Ever since I knew it to be scientifically true, I had seen Jude in a new light. Now I saw things we had in common. Now that I had permission to believe it, I found that I noticed all sorts of things that were similar.

"Do you have a sister?" I asked, getting recklessly close to telling him the truth as we walked through the quiet kitchen together. I saw a cake box on the counter, and I tried to think about Alex and his birthday, but my brain kept pushing me to think about telling Jude he was my brother. That was why Alex had pushed me out here, after all. He wanted me to come clean. I felt a wave of anticipation at the thought that I might tell him.

"I do have a sister," Jude said. "Liv. Olivia. She lives in Philadelphia."

"Any kids?"

"Two. Both girls. Both little. Two and under. The baby's just a few months older than Ben."

"Wow, babies everywhere," I said. "You must really love your dad if you named Ben after him."

"I do," Jude said. "He's up in Philadelphia and I only see him once or twice a year, but yeah. I wouldn't be who I am without my dad. And we liked the name. It's on Andy's side, too. Her grandfather. Oh, my goodness, I cannot believe this truck," Jude said as we walked out of the kitchen and down the path that led to a small parking lot near the service entrance of their kitchen. There were four or five vehicles parked in a neat row, and Alex's new truck was the first one we came to.

Jude pressed the button to unlock the door and then reached out and opened it. He stood back and offered to let me get into the driver's seat.

"You go ahead," I said. "I'll be riding in it a bunch."

Jude sat in the seat. "You must really like Alex."

"I can't even believe how much I like him," I said. "I didn't think twice about getting him this truck. He deserves it."

"He does. You're right. Alex is awesome. It's just crazy how you... it's crazy that Lindsay already ordered your new book. Magnolia something?"

"Magnolia Borderlands," I said.

"What's the name about?"

"Well, it's a fictional place—a post-apocalyptic reality. As far as naming it magnolia... I don't know. Magnolia is a nostalgic word for me. I don't know why. The book's set in a landscape I picture as the old American south, and the magnolia is one of the most endearing southern symbols for me. They're big and have strong, sturdy flowers. And I just love the smell of them. Once I figured out the premise and setting of the book, it was a no brainer that I'd call the borderlands magnolia."

"I love magnolias, too," Jude said. "Trees in general, but magnolias are cool. There's a lot of them on the farm. Andy and I have two on our property. Alex might have a few of them, too. I'm always picking them for Andy. They usually quit blooming by now, but the trees we have bloom into the fall. So do the ones at the end of the driveway, here. I bet we could find a flower if we went over there."

"In October?" I asked even though I didn't know much about it.

"I swear they bloom this late," Jude said. "I bet we can find a bloom on one of the trees at the end of this driveway. It's sporadic, but I've definitely seen them lately. Hop in and we'll take Alex's truck for a spin—we'll go get you one."

I ran around to the passenger's side and jumped into the truck with Jude.

"We'll just go to the end of the driveway," he said. "Alex won't mind. Oh, wow, this is so nice," he continued, checking everything out as he backed out of the spot and slowly drove down the driveway. "I'm gonna have to look into one of these, myself."

Jude drove right up to the magnolia tree, parking the truck so he could get out.

"It's got two on it that I can see," he said pointing up at one of the trees. "I don't know if I can reach them."

"You don't have to," I said. "I think it's just cool that one's blooming this late. Just seeing it…"

"Oh, I'll try to get it for you," Jude said, opening his truck door. "We gotta get you an Autumn magnolia." He smiled, looking proud of himself for making the joke. "Get it?" he said. "It works both ways."

"Yes, I get it," I said, shaking my head at him.

Jude jogged across the twenty feet of grass to get to the magnolia tree. There were two big trees at the end of the driveway. One of them had no visible blooms, but this one had a couple of lone flowers. Jude went underneath the tree, jumping up and grabbing on to a branch. I hadn't expected him to do any of this and I covered my mouth with my hand as I watched him jump.

He came down with a flower—one I hadn't even seen from where I was standing. I had gotten out of the truck, but I stayed close to it with the door open instead of following Jude over to the tree. He ran the half-opened white blossom back to me. He was a grown man, and yet I could see the little kid in him as he brought me that flower. He knew I wanted it, and he was proud to be the one to deliver it. It was overwhelmingly endearing, and I smiled and took it from Jude, feeling like my heart was about to burst. I buried my nose in the white flower the instant it was in my possession. It was chilly out and the petals were cool to the touch. My nose rested on the cool velvet surface as I took in its sweet perfume.

"Sooo good," I said, feeling genuinely happy in that moment. "Thank you."

Jude grinned and started to move to go back to the driver's side of the truck, but I called his name. "Jude, wait."

He stopped. "Yeah?"

"Thank you for getting this," I said.

He smiled. "You're welcome. I'm glad we found one I could reach."

He started to move again, but I stopped him.

"And, Jude?"

"Yeah?"

"Do you think I could tell you something?"

"Sure. Of course. Whatcha got?"

"The thing is," I said, glancing around even though no one was there. "I have to ask you not to tell anyone. I'd like to share something with you and I'd like it to stay between us. Can that happen?"

"Okay," he said, trying to be accommodating, but now looking slightly concerned.

I felt nervous. Part of me regretted getting myself into this situation. But there I was. I already had him engaged, interested. And now I had to make a choice. I needed to go ahead and spit it out or tell him never mind.

"My dad is a writer," I said.

"I heard," he said, since we had just talked about it at dinner.

"He and my mom, well, they… got a divorce when I was in high school, but they were together my whole life."

"Oh, that's good they made it that long," Jude said, being nice.

"Yeah. I don't know if you heard me say, but my mom passed away recently."

"Yeah, I did. I'm sorry to hear about that." Jude was being friendly and accommodating, but I could tell had no idea why I would want to stand in the driveway and strike up a deep conversation. He was being patient, though, not rushing me.

I took a deep breath. "My mom, before she died, she wrote this letter."

My heart was pounding, and I transferred the flower to my left hand so that I could use my right to cover my chest. I had to make sure my heart didn't jump out. I took another calming breath.

"There was this part in the letter, the whole letter, actually, that was the point of it, but it was about my dad not being my real dad, and well, my mom, she named names about who my real d-dad could be, and, well, even though we have a piece of information doesn't mean we have to… look, I know you're all situated over here, and I'm not, I would never try to do anything to disrupt your… I'm not trying to come in and be a part of… besides, it would kill my dad, Amos, to know any of this. He doesn't even know, and he would... I don't want him to know, for sure."

Jude's expression was serious, concerned, and confused as he stared at me. I realized I was rambling and not doing a great job of putting my thoughts into words, but he didn't seem like he understood me at all. I paused and looked at him with a regretful expression.

"I'm sorry," I said. "Thank you for getting me this flower. I love it. I loved how you jumped up there and snatched it."

"Whoa, whoa, whoa, back up. You can't just... what were you saying a second ago? You were talking about your mom and a letter, and then you said you didn't want to come here and disrupt me."

"Yeah," I said, agreeing with his summary.

He leveled me with a cautious glance. "Yeah, but it feels like part of this story is missing." He was staring straight at me with a serious expression, waiting for me to say something.

"It's just, I didn't come here trying to—"

"What are you saying, Autumn?" he asked.

The question was direct. His expression was intense, and I felt I had no other choice but to speak plainly.

"I think... I'm pretty sure... your dad is my dad. At least, by blood or whatever."

I was still getting out the last word when Jude rushed me, taking me into his arms. I was not expecting it, and I stiffened out a little before I could get comfortable and hug him back. I thought he would let me go right away, but he stayed there and held me, hugged me.

Relief and happiness flooded my body, making it impossible for me to hold back tears. I held onto Jude, my brother, crying and doing my best to hold back sobs. He hugged me for several long seconds before pulling back to stare at me.

He put his hands on the side of my face, holding nothing back, displaying blatant, unrepentant curiosity. Jude stared at me like the apes on Tarzan when they found a baby. He let me go and took a step back, staring and shaking his head in wonder.

I smiled, using the back of my hand to wipe away tears.

"Are you really?" he asked.

"I mean, yeah, I'm definitely Ezekiel's niece. I took a piece of his hair off of his collar and turned it in to a medical lab. It's shows that we're… uncle-niece, or whatever. He doesn't even know I did that. Everyone thinks I'm just a writer, which I am. But I wasn't here doing book research. My mom told me the name of my biological dad, and I… I don't want to disrupt anyone's lives."

"Stop saying you're disrupting things. You're not. It's amazing. I can't believe it. Did you say your dad is Ben Tanner? Does Alex know?"

"Yes, I said that. And Alex definitely knows."

"That boy knew I had a sister? For how long?"

"I don't know, weeks. I told him right when I found out it was true."

"I can't believe he didn't tell me," Jude said, shaking his head.

"I begged him not to," I said. "It's not his fault. He really wanted me to tell you, but I wasn't ready. That's why he told me to walk outside with you just now. He wanted us to be alone. He wanted to tempt me."

"So, Uncle E doesn't know? Aunt Rhonda?"

"No."

"What about my dad?"

"No. Definitely not. I've never even seen him or talked to him. Just Alex knows. And my friend from California. And my mom's lawyer."

Jude gave me an easy smile. "Are you seriously my sister? I feel like you're joking me right now. I can't even take it in."

I let out a laugh. "Welcome to the club," I said. "The last month of my life has been one surreal experience after another."

"You have to let me tell Liv. I have to tell Dad. And uncle E. We have to tell everyone."

"No, no, no, no, no, no, no. We don't need to do that. Let's just take it one Tanner at a time, okay?"

Jude put his arm around my shoulder and began walking me to the truck. He carried himself with a certain confidence like everything was going to be okay.

"You're scaring me with how quick we're going back," I said.

"Yeah, if I don't go back now, everyone will wonder what's going on."

"Good, yes, good, good plan," I said, getting into the passenger's side.

Jude ran to the driver's side, and started the truck. He turned around and headed back down the driveway the way we came. We were quiet for the first few seconds. I smelled the magnolia, and that mixed with the leathery new car smell of the truck made me feel soothed and comfortable.

"So, you're not going to say anything?" I asked.

"Not right this second," he said. "But you can bet I'm telling my wife, and then I'm sure I'll have to tell Dad and Liv and the rest of them eventually, if you don't do it."

He glanced at me from over the console. "Your dad won't find out," he said, reassuring me. "I understand that it would be an issue for him. I'll be careful. I'm not trying to jeopardize your family over there. I'm just really glad I know, Autumn. This is awesome news for us. I want to be able to love you and have you be my sister, even if we can't go telling the world. And Dad, Uncle E, Liv… they'll all feel that same way."

Stinging tears sprang to my eyes again, and I had to lean forward and adjust the air conditioner so that it would blow in my face.

Chapter 18

Alex

"What are they doing?" Jordan said, craning his neck to peer out of the window. The living room windows faced a section of the driveway, and Jordan caught sight of Alex's truck as Jude drove it. The windows were tinted, but the sun was low in the sky and shining just right, and he saw two people.

"What's going on?" Rhonda asked, since she couldn't see the driveway from where she was sitting.

Jordan stood up. "He's parking down at the end of the driveway."

"He's probably showing Autumn something about the farm," Alex said. "She's always asking questions. And I'm glad they test drove the truck."

He wanted Jude and Autumn to spend time together. He didn't care where they were going or what they were doing. He hoped the excursion resulted in Autumn telling Jude the truth.

"Yeah, I bet Jude wanted to drive that truck," Jordan agreed. "You better watch out, Andy. He'll be truck shopping tonight on the internet."

"What is that boy doing?" Andy said, peering outside. "He was supposed to bring me a diaper."

"Just use one of Wolfie's," Jordan offered. "They're size four, but you can strap it tight. You know, cinch it up."

"I'm sure I have some smaller ones," Rhonda said. "Just go look in the nursery. I know for sure I have some in there."

"Yeah, she probably has some in the nursery." Alex agreed, hoping they would give Jude and Autumn some space.

Andy stood up and took little Ben to the nursery. Considering the fact that it was slightly odd for her husband to drive away in Alex's truck with Alex's new famous girlfriend, Andy did a great job of brushing it off and knowing she could ultimately trust Jude.

Everyone was a little curious as to why they had taken off, but no one actively watched them. They were far enough away that everyone sort of went back to what they were doing.

Alex kept the conversation going, talking about Autumn's curiosity, which led to them talking about her book and how unbelievable it was that Alex had met her and scooped her up at the farm. They talked about the truck, and how much she must like Alex to have bought it.

Alex tried not to make it obvious, but he watched Jude and Autumn like a hawk, and he got nervous every time someone glanced out of the window. After a minute, he saw Jude and Autumn embrace. Jordan looked that way right when it happened, and it caused Alex to choke on his drink. He managed not to spill, but he coughed violently, burying his head in his shirt and coughing to clear his airway. He was desperate to keep everyone from looking out of the window, and he held up a finger, widening his eyes between coughs like he wanted to say something even though he was actively choking.

"Oh gosh, hang on," he said, finally. His choking had been an accidental distraction, but it kept everyone temporarily from looking out of the window. Even the babies were looking at him. Alex worked his way through the coughing fit, holding his hand up like he really needed to say something.

"I was going to ask when we were doing cake," Alex said, once he finally quit coughing. It was a ridiculous thing to say, but it was the first thing that came to his mind.

"Hungry, champ?" Jordan said, teasing Alex. "You might want to take a minute after that little coughing fit you had there."

"You know I only get that German chocolate once a year on my birthday," Alex said, acting serious even though it was only a distraction. None of this had anything to do with cake. He was looking forward to the German chocolate, and he would enjoy it, but he was more concentrating on keeping everyone from looking out of the window.

Thankfully, Jude and Autumn got back into the truck and headed up the driveway again. They made their way into the living room at the same time that

Andy and the baby came in from the other direction. Everyone approached the coffee table at the same time.

"Where'd you go?" Rhonda asked.

"Autumn and I were talking about magnolias and I told her these trees will bloom into the fall. I knew that one at the end of the driveway had a couple flowers, so I used the excuse to drive Alex's truck."

"Still doesn't seem like it's mine," Alex said, shrugging and looking unaffected.

"Did you find one?" Rhonda asked. "A flower?"

Autumn lifted her hand, displaying the small white blossom.

"Oh, good. I didn't even notice that was on there. Jude always notices things like that."

Autumn made eye contact with Alex on her way to him. He smiled at her. She was the most beautiful thing he had ever seen. It had been weeks, and he missed her like crazy. It was unbelievable to Alex that she was in the same room as him. She walked straight over to him, smiling and assuming she would sit where she had been before. Alex made room for her.

Jude and Andy had an exchange about how it was a good thing Andy had taken care of Ben in the nursery because Jude forgot the diaper bag after all. Everyone gave Jude a hard time about that and he blamed it on being distracted by Alex's new truck.

Alex could tell that Autumn had told Jude. They had come into the room with a countenance that had changed. Both of them had on a nostalgic smile like they were seeing everything through rose colored glasses.

Alex pulled Autumn close to him the second she sat down. They took a few seconds to have a private conversation while everyone was ribbing Jude about forgetting the diaper bag.

"How'd it go?" he asked in hushed tones.

"Good. I told him," she responded.

"I knew it," Alex said. "Are you telling everyone?"

"Not yet," she said. "Not tonight. I'm already on the verge of a heart attack from saying it once. And I have to figure things out with Dad. My dad. Amos."

Alex nodded, knowing they didn't have any more time to carry on a private conversation while everyone else was talking to each other. He wanted her close to him, he wished it were proper to have her on his lap. He had to fight against the urge to pull her over to him. He made light contact with her any time he could. She was adorable, irresistible. Her dark eyes called to him.

He could tell just by how she looked at him that she loved him back. She had come there because she loved him. He could see it in her eyes.

The whole family sang Happy Birthday to Alex and everyone got a piece of chocolate cake. Justin, Zeke, and their crews were the first families to leave once they were finished with dessert. They all had young babies and were on a strict evening routine.

Jordan and Mica stayed a little longer and so did Jude and Andy. They talked about obvious things like horse racing and basketball, and they also talked about movies, music, and pop culture.

Alex kept Autumn close to him the whole time, and he could tell that was where she wanted to be. "We're heading back to the oasis," Ezekiel said, referring to his bedroom.

"Yeah, you guys stay as long as you like." Rhonda said.

"Night!" Jordan said. "We'll be leaving soon."

"You're not bothering us," she assured him, giving hugs to everyone one-by-one.

"Night," Alex said, hugging Rhonda. "Thank you for everything tonight. Seriously, I'm still processing."

"Well, we love you, kid," she said, reaching up to pinch his cheek.

"I love y'all too," Alex said.

"We love y'all too," Mica said. "We're gonna take off so we can get this baby fed and in bed."

Everyone hugged, but Alex and Autumn didn't mention leaving right away and neither did Jude or Andy.

"I might have one more slice of that cake before we go," Jude said.

"There's plenty," Alex said. "Help yourself."

"Andy, let Autumn hold Ben for a minute. Come over here and eat some cake with me," Jude said once everyone else had left.

Andy looked at Autumn with a hopeful expression. "If you don't mind," she said.

"I don't mind at all," Autumn said. "I was going to ask about holding him earlier, but I wanted to make sure everybody had a turn."

Alex and Autumn took a seat on a small couch that was lining the wall in the kitchen area. She snuggled up next to him, and Andy came over, unhooking the baby holding device that was strapped to her front and carefully delivering the precious package to Autumn.

"Oh, he's awake," Autumn said in an excited whisper.

"Oh yeah he's been awake. He's just been chillin', looking around."

"She's my sister," Jude announced from across the kitchen. "I'm sorry, but it's just us, and Autumn knew I was going to tell Andy anyway, and well, I didn't want to wait. I couldn't wait. I think it's a great time to say it."

"What in the world are you talking about?" Andy asked, looking at Jude like he had lost his mind.

Autumn tensed as she waited for Jude to repeat himself. Alex could feel her go rigid, and he put a hand on her leg, comforting her, holding her steady. She glanced at him with a thankful smile.

"My sister is Autumn," Jude said, cutting a slice of cake. "Autumn is my sister."

"Why are you saying that?" Andy asked, staring at him.

"Because she is. Apparently, her mother and our father knew each other, back twenty-five-years-or-so-ago. How old are you?" Jude asked.

"Twenty-five," Autumn said.

"The youngest of us," Jude said. "I'm twenty-seven and Liv's... how old is Liv? She's at least thirty, maybe thirty-one."

"Are y'all messing with me?" Andy asked, still looking confused. "Because it's getting late, and I have mom brain right now."

"I'm being a hundred percent serious," Jude said. "Unless she's messing with me."

"I'm not," Autumn said.

"She's my sister. For real. Half-sister. Ben's her dad."

Alex felt Autumn squirm when he said that. She squinted and rubbed her eyes, trying not to cry before focusing on baby Ben's perfect little face.

"When did you find out about this?" Andy asked.

"Alex knew about it, but I just found out a little while ago when we drove down to the end of the driveway. She said her real dad, her other dad, the one in California, has no idea, so we can't go telling everybody we meet or anything."

"I wouldn't tell anyone," Andy said. "But oh my goodness. Is it for real? Does Ezekiel know? Does Ben know?"

"No. No one knows. No one but Alex and us."

Andy had initially been making her way to Jude, but she turned around and heading back toward Autumn, staring at her with fascination.

"So, you knew this when you came here the first time?" she asked.

Autumn nodded. She had the baby cradled in her arms securely enough that she felt comfortable looking at Andy.

Alex put his hand on her leg for support, but she didn't need it. She was surprised by the confrontation but comfortable and confident at the same time. She leaned into Alex as she smiled at Andy.

"You know, I do see little Tanner elements in her," Andy said, moving closer, inspecting Autumn's face carefully. "Maybe some Liv, and even Stella. You see that, in the mouth?"

"I know. I was thinking that when she smiled a few minutes ago," Jude said.

Autumn blushed as a result of the close examination, and Alex thought it was the most beautiful thing he had ever seen.

Chapter 19

Autumn

It was Friday, and Alex only had to work until 3pm. Yesterday was Alex's birthday, and tomorrow would be the big Tanner basketball banquet, but today was low-key. I got up early and did some work from my hotel room, and then Jude's wife, Andy, picked me up for lunch.

We ate at a casual restaurant and then went back to their house. It was the place she and Jude had built on the outskirts of the Tanner farm. As we drove onto the property, she explained about Alex's lot, pointing out where it was and explaining where he would likely build a house. Their property backed up to the farm, and they had direct access to it, but they were situated on their own road.

I had been to the farm, obviously, but never to this side of it. It was beautiful and serene—more wooded than I expected after seeing the big open pastures in the middle of the farm.

Andy loved me instantly. She embraced me as Jude's sister and wanted to spend time with me and get to know me. She was fun, and little Ben was a good baby. Our time together that afternoon was natural and easy. We visited at their house for a while after lunch, and then she took me to Stella's since I hadn't met her yet.

Stella and Caleb were the ones who had a three-year-old boy named Amos. It was a little surreal, meeting a boy with the same name as my dad since it was such a rare name and I never heard it.

Caleb was there for a few minutes, and I got to meet him as well. Andy didn't tell either of them about my true identity while we were there. Stella had heard enough about me by then to know about me being a writer, but she didn't seem to know anything about my identity as a Tanner, and Andy, although she had to catch herself one time, didn't mention it.

I could see myself in Stella's smile, though, which was surreal. There were a few times that she made certain expressions and I had to look away.

Alex got off work at three that afternoon. I was still hanging out with Andy and Stella and had lost track of time when my phone rang. We were standing in the kitchen, and I was holding Ben. My phone happened to be sitting on the counter near Stella, and she looked at me after glancing at it.

"Alex," she said.

"Oh, dang," I said, glancing around for a clock.

"I'll take Benjamin," Andy said.

"Can I answer it?" Stella asked.

"Sure," I said.

"Hey, Alex, it's Stella. I didn't get to see you yesterday on your birthday, so happy birthday!"

"Thank you, Stella," I heard him say, plain as day. My phone was not on speakerphone, but his voice projected over the regular speaker quite nicely. I handed Ben back to his mom in preparation to talk to Alex.

"I met your new lady friend," Stella said to him.

"I guess you did, since you picked up her phone," Alex replied.

Stella glanced at me, but I could tell she didn't think I could hear Alex. "She's right here. She and Andy came over."

"Ask her what she wants me to do right now," Alex said. "Come over there, or see her later."

"What do you want him to do?" Stella asked, looking at me and having no idea I had heard Alex. "What do you want to do?" Stella asked Alex before I had the chance to answer.

"I want to... see her as soon as possible," Alex said in that serious but lighthearted voice.

I kept my expression under control, trying not to react, trying to pretend I couldn't hear him.

Stella smiled at me. "You should come over," she said to Alex. "She rode over here with Andy, so I'm sure you could kidnap her if you want to."

"I definitely want to kidnap her," Alex said. "Tell her I'm on my way."

"Do you need to talk to her?" Stella asked.

"No. Just tell her I'll be there in ten minutes."

"Okay," Stella said. She hung up my phone. "That was Alex," she added.

"We figured," Andy said, swaying and patting Ben's butt.

"He's on his way, and he liiiiikes you, Autumn." Stella's eyes widened as she said that. She was talking directly to me.

"Oh, you should see them together, they are so cute," Andy said.

I was already wound up from hearing Alex say he was coming to kidnap me, and now they were making me blush.

"Oh, my gosh, y'all are in love, huh?" Stella said, looking at my reaction to all of this.

I put my hand over my face, knowing I had turned pink and unable to do anything about it. "I like him so much," I said. "I mean, I have a whole life, and friends, and commitments in California… an apartment. I can't be here right now, and yet, here I am, setting up camp in a hotel in Kentucky. Three months ago, I would have never dreamed I'd be… feeling compelled to follow a guy across the country." I delivered the statement in a comically dazed tone that made them laugh. "And there's even more to the story that I haven't told you, Stella."

"What? Are y'all getting married?" she asked. "Did you already get married?"

"No, no, nothing like that, although, I could see us… no… that's not what I'm saying. I didn't plan on telling anyone at all about this, so it's comical how many know. I just keep adding and adding people to the list."

"It's going to have to end up being everybody," Andy said.

"I know," I said to her. "I didn't realize it would be so awkward trying to get to know everyone and not mention it. Especially now... since you and Jude know."

"Y'all are freaking me out," Stella said. "What in the world is going on?"

"Ben Tanner, your uncle, has a daughter named Autumn, and this is her right here."

"Wait." Stella's hand instantly went to her face, shielding it like she might cry. "What?"

"Autumn is your cousin," Andy said, since Stella and I were both kind of speechless. "Her mom told her about it, but her dad doesn't know, so don't post it on the internet or anything. But yes, she's Jude's sister. Ben's daughter."

"Why did he not tell us about you?" Stella asked. She bent down to pick up Amos, who was lifting his arms, waiting for her. She stood with him and settled him on her hip.

"I came here to try to discreetly meet my biological family," I said. "From a distance. It's not unheard of for me to travel for book research, but this time, I said I wanted to work on a horse farm. I knew quite a few Tanners were working here, and I figured that would be a nice way to meet everybody from a distance without hurting my dad or disrupting anyone's lives. I was not planning on telling anyone about it."

"And everything would have gone according to plan if you hadn't fallen in love." Stella said it as a statement and not a question.

"Exactly," I said. "I can't seem to leave that boy alone."

"Why would you want to?" Andy asked. "Alex is a huge catch."

"He seriously is," Stella said. "I'm not even joking about his size. Seriously, I'm not just trying to say this to make you jealous, but every one of my single teacher friends wants to be set up with him."

"That *is* making me jealous," I said, joking around and causing them to laugh.

"He loves her," Andy said.

"I can tell already," Stella said. "Besides, Alex has been around long enough that he had the chance to go out with them by now if he wanted to. I was just saying what a catch he was." Stella smiled absentmindedly at me while holding Amos on her hip. "This seems like a lot of information to take in at once," she said. "I'm so happy about you and Alex, and I think that's amazing, but I am freaking out about you being my cousin. Who all knows? I feel like we need to celebrate or something."

Alex knocked on the door a few minutes later. Amos and Stella walked over to answer it, and I waited with Andy in the kitchen. I heard them having a conversation at the foyer, but I couldn't hear what they were saying.

Alex came around the corner wearing jeans and a button-down shirt. I didn't see him when he left for work that morning, so I didn't know what he had on. He normally wore athletic attire to work. Technically, his uniform pants qualified as sweats, but they were the high-class version of them. Alex was always really professional and polished looking.

"What cha dressed up for?" Andy asked, noticing the jeans.

"I had lunch with the Dean today," Alex said.

He walked toward me, and I felt like I wanted to burst into a fit of giggles. He was something wonderful. I was so relived to be in Lexington with him. I wanted to never be apart from him again.

I watched as he paused and greeted Andy and Ben for a second before making his way over to me. He smiled and came in for the kiss the instant he walked up to me. I stretched up and kissed him back, and we hugged before he settled in behind me. We were standing in the kitchen, and he casually leaned on the counter, pulling me close.

"I like your shirt," I said. It was a white shirt with small blue checks. He was dapper looking in dark jeans, and the whole package made my heart race.

"Friday's spirit day," Alex said. "Gotta have my blue and white."

"You have blue and white every day," Stella said, teasing him and making us all laugh.

I loved what he was wearing. I wanted to buy him clothes. I wanted to take care of him. I was unaccustomed to all the urges I felt with Alex. He reached out and held my hand, lacing his fingers in mine.

"Do you want something to drink?" Stella asked him.

"Whatcha got?" he asked.

"Iced tea. Or I could make a pot of coffee. Always water or milk."

"A drink would be great," Alex said. "Thank you, Stella."

"Which one?"

"Iced tea."

Stella crossed the kitchen to make Alex a drink, and Amos got distracted and went to play with his toys in the living room.

"I can get it," Alex said.

"That's okay," Stella said. "I know right where everything is."

She looked at Alex when she came to stand next to us. "Your girlfriend is my cousin," she said. She made a face. "That's the last sentence I thought I'd be saying today," she added.

"She told you?" Alex said, wearing an easy smile. He looked at me. "Before long, everybody'll know."

"I know, I'm kind of seeing that. But I have to do it at my own pace, and natural. Like I was just sitting here with Stella, and it came out. I don't want to go telling everybody right now with them thinking about the banquet and everything. We still have all the time in the world. I'm sure I will, but I want to let it happen naturally."

"How long are you staying here?" Stella asked.

"I bought a one way for now because I wasn't sure."

"Days? Weeks?" Andy asked.

"Yeah," I said.

"You shouldn't be in a hotel." Stella said. "I mean, unless you just really want to. But, we all have room. You have, like, five houses you could stay at while you're here. Uncle E and Aunt Rhonda have that whole back part of the house they never even use. They'd love to have you."

"They offered," I said. "But I told them I was fine at the hotel. I already had the reservation, and I sprang the visit on them in the first place."

"Well, you know if they find out about the other…" Stella said. "I mean, they'd do anything for you now, but just wait till they find out. Spoiled rotten."

"Oh, I don't need to be spoiled," I said. "I'm just happy that you guys… it's a relief that you guys know about it and don't think I'm trying to come over here and…" I hesitated and paused, not wanting to say the wrong thing. "I'm really happy, that's all. I'm happy you guys are so nice."

Chapter 20

Alex picked me up at the hotel. I wore a gray dress that I had brought with me from California. I didn't want to accidently choose the color of their arch rival team. I didn't even know if that was a thing, but I thought gray would be neutral.

Alex was insatiable from the time he came to pick me up. He loved how I looked in the dress. He kept reaching out for me and pulling me close. He talked about my appearance and tried to get close to me and kiss me. I loved it. I pretended to protest and try to keep him at bay, but he knew I loved it.

The Tanner house was huge, and it was full of people on the night of the banquet. It was an official event. They hired help. Catering and other service companies were parked in the back with vans and other vehicles taking up the whole back entrance. Alex and I ended up using the valet.

Alex put his hand on my back as we walked toward the door. He messed with the fabric of my dress. It tickled, and I squirmed and looked at him, making him smile at me like I was in trouble. I told him I was too nervous to flirt and that I had to suck in my gut and worry about meeting new people. I told him I couldn't stop to be lovey-dovey with him, but really, I was flirting with him by pretending I shouldn't flirt, and he knew that.

We were constantly staring at each other, sharing conspiratorial expressions and making subtle bodily contacts. I reached for Alex's hand, pulling his arm in front of me and into my grasp. He wasn't wearing a tie, but he had on dress pants and a matching jacket. It was navy, and he wore it with a powder blue shirt. I had picked the combination out of his closet the night before. He had two nice suits, and I already had plans to get him at least one more.

I had never experienced the urge to buy a guy things the way I did with Alex. I felt compelled to shower him with gifts. I had never felt this way about anyone before, but it gave me pleasure to buy him things. As we walked toward the house, I held onto Alex's arm, feeling proud and happy.

The first people we encountered were members of the current UK team. Several players and their families were in the big ballroom area near the entrance, and we stopped with four or five different groups so that Alex could greet them and introduce me.

The room had been transformed with gorgeous round tables that had linens and centerpieces. There was a live jazz band set up on the other side of the room, and people were standing around or finding a seat at a table.

What got me was how close Alex was to all of the players. He wasn't just their physical therapist. I got the impression, by the things they said to him, that he was a teammate and friend. They did these handshakes that were slightly more complex than a normal greeting with him. I could just tell they were close. They talked him up to me, saying how he played basketball with them all the time and how he "had skills for an old man" and other things like that. The team admired and respected Alex—that was obvious to me as soon as I met all of them. What was even cooler than that, was that they didn't know me as a writer, or even as Ezekiel's niece. All they knew about me was that I was there with Alex, and they respected me for it.

We spent ten or fifteen minutes in the ballroom area, talking to members of the team. I had seen Jordan from a distance, but he was talking to someone as they walked through the corner of the room, heading toward that blue living room where we had been the other night. I hadn't seen anyone else in the family. I still hadn't met Tanner or his parents, Sara and Ricky. I had seen their pictures, and I heard they would be there tonight, but we hadn't run into them yet.

"Where's the family?" I asked Alex when we finished talking to one of the players, a guy named Gabe.

"They're probably in the kitchen or in the living room with the game on," Alex said. "People kind of all spread out at this thing. I bet the family's in there watching the game."

I knew he was talking about the UK football game, which was also happening that night.

"I think that's where Jordan went a minute ago," I said. "I saw him come through here and go that way."

"Yeah, I bet there's a lot of people back there. We can go see, if you want."

Alex put his hand on my back. It was warm, and I loved it there, but I wanted him even closer. I reached behind me and wrapped his arm all the way around me. I felt compelled to constantly remind him how much I liked him. I was walking beside Alex and trying to put words to the glorious feeling of butterflies when Jude rushed up to us, startling me.

"Hey, oh, good, you didn't… did you? How long have you been here? At this party?" He seemed rushed and nervous.

I had been looking down and I hadn't seen Jude approach us in the hallway, so it took me a second to try to take in what he was saying. I tried to think about his words, but I couldn't make much sense of it. I was about to ask him to repeat himself when Alex spoke up.

"We just got here like ten or fifteen minutes ago," Alex said.

"Oh, no, really? That long? I thought you would come in through the… kitchen. I was back there, waiting for you."

"We used the valet," Alex said. "The back lot and the driveway were full when we got here."

Jude took a deep breath and looked around. "Have you seen anyone?"

"Just Gabe and Richie and them—a few of the other sophomores, back in the front room, why?"

Jude looked back and forth from Alex to me before leveling me with a sincere stare. "Well, Autumn, first of all, you look beautiful tonight. Your dress is really pretty. And you're really pretty. I like your hair. Second. This is… I told Uncle E. I'm so sorry. I'm really sorry. But you're my sister, and I'm excited about it. I was with him yesterday, and we were talking about you, and it just came out. I didn't intend to do it, but I did. I'm sorry, but he knows. I love you, and I'm excited. Which brings me to my third thing. I did not tell him. He does not know. Uncle E knows, but Dad does not. But he is here. Dad, I mean. First, let me say, I had no idea he would actually come. Me and Uncle E called him last night and said he should drive down here for the banquet, and he took us up on it. We told him it was Tanner's last banquet as a college player, and that he could see little Ben. Long story short is that he showed up. He's here. We honestly didn't think he would come, but he drove here. But like I said, he doesn't know anything. We didn't tell him."

Jude paused and took a deep breath after all that talking. His expression had been a little worried looking the whole time he spoke, but once he paused, he made a pitiful face like *please forgive me.*

"I did tell Uncle E, and I did invite Dad. I know Aunt Rhonda knows about you, too, because you know, Uncle E told her. None of us told Dad, though."

Jude sighed and reached out and took me into his arms, and I let go of Alex long enough to hug him back.

"I love you," he said, his deep voice sounding loud with my ear near his chest. "I didn't mean to do anything behind your back, but we love you, Autumn. Uncle E was pumped when I told him. We're all so happy about everything."

Chapter 21

I stared at the marble floors and the window treatments, and anything that could distract me from the flood of tears that threatened to fill my eyes.

My biological father was in the house.

It was difficult to decipher all of the emotions I was feeling at the moment… relief, hope, fear, embarrassment, happiness, dread, elation.

"I'm happy too," I said breathlessly to Jude, trying to ignore all of the other feelings.

"We would have called you to give you a heads up on all of this, but Uncle E was just going to wait till he could see you face-to-face and talk to you about it. You know, hug your neck and everything. And we didn't even know Dad was coming until this afternoon. He didn't call till he was already on his way."

I could tell Jude was worried that I'd be mad at him. This whole encounter was a little shocking, but I didn't feel mad at him.

"It's okay," I said, trying to breathe steadily and get a hold of my emotions. "I told Stella about it yesterday."

"I know," Jude said, nodding. "Andy told me. That made me feel better about telling Uncle E." Jude regarded me sincerely. "I really did mean to keep it a secret until you told him yourself, but I was with him all day yesterday, and you came up. It just came out."

"It's fine," I said. "I had resolved to tell everybody, anyway. I don't think my dad would ever find out, even if all of you guys knew about it. He's kind of in his own world in California."

"Yeah, and Dad doesn't know anybody," Jude agreed. "He wouldn't go around telling anybody or try to hurt your… dad."

"Oh, I know," I said even though it was good to hear him say that. I regarded Jude with a reluctant expression. "But are you sure he would even want to know?"

"Absolutely," Jude said with no hesitation at all. "You mean my dad, our dad, Ben? Yes. A hundred percent. He would a hundred percent want to know."

We were positioned in a corner between the ballroom and the hall. Several people walked by as we were standing there, and Alex and Jude both waved, but I didn't know any of them, and they could see we were talking.

And then, there he was.

I just knew it.

It was a group of three gentlemen, Ezekiel, Ben, and Tanner. They were heading from the living room like they planned on walking past us. Ezekiel's eyes locked with mine as he steered them our way, walking right up to us. He gave me a warm smile as he approached, and his expression shifted where he was telling me he knew who I was. His eyes were full of kindness and love, and I blinked, holding back tears and trying to calm my nerves. They came to a stop near us.

"I know you've met Ezekiel," Alex said, taking over, talking to me. "But this is Tanner, Ezekiel's nephew, and Ben, Ezekiel's brother, from Philadelphia. This is Autumn."

Tanner did some kind of handshake with Alex, smiling in that sideways, sly confident way star athletes did. "Bro, Gabe already texted me that you had your lady with you tonight. Congrats, brother." He winked mischievously at Alex, but then he schooled his expression and regarded me with one that was more gentlemanly. "Nice to meet you, Autumn."

"You too, Tanner," I said.

"You'll have to excuse me. I'm just giving Alex a hard time. We heard he had a lady in California, but I can't say we believed him too much. He wouldn't tell us anything about you other than he was in looooove." Tanner said it dramatically, teasing Alex.

I glanced up at Alex. "Thank goodness he is," I said, causing them to laugh.

"Hey, seriously, it was nice to meet you, Autumn. I'm gonna see you over here at the table in a minute. Coach is trying to get me over there to talk to somebody."

"Go ahead and go to Coach," Ezekiel said. "We'll meet you over there."

Tanner nodded and told us all goodbye. He gave Alex an exaggerated thumbs up, telling him he had done good with me, which made me smile.

"California, huh? What part?" Ben was the one who had asked me the question.

It was difficult to make eye contact with him, but I made myself. "Los…" I cleared my throat. "Los Angeles."

"Autumn is a successful writer," Ezekiel said.

"No kidding. Like Stephen King?"

"One can dream," I said.

"She is," Ezekiel said. "The girls had all read her books before they even met her."

"Well, isn't that something," Ben said, looking impressed. "My girlfriend reads. Maybe I should get your autograph."

He seemed open and impressed, and I used the opportunity to just… say it. "Uh, Mister Tanner, I, uh, do you happen to, years ago, maybe, remember a woman named Kate Hanson? It would have been like twenty-five years ago or so."

I must have sounded nervous or scared because Alex came up behind me like a wall, taking me into his arms, wrapping himself around me like a physical fortress.

Ben made a sincere face like he was doing his best to follow me but not quite succeeding.

"I think it was in Charlotte, North Carolina," I said, feeling calmer and more comfortable now, thanks to Alex's embrace. "It would have been a long time ago. You might have been there watching Mister Ezekiel play basketball against the Charlotte Hornets. I think my mom was there for a gymnastics competition, and you guys were in the same hotel or something."

"Oh, my goodness, yes! North Carolina. What did you say her name was? I remember that, I sure do. Did you say that lady was your mom?" He stared at me intently, scanning my face, looking like he was trying to remember. "Goodness, I see it now. You look a lot like your mother. Beautiful lady." He spoke slowly and stared at me, still inspecting my face. "What'd you say her name was?" he asked absentmindedly.

"Kate Hanson."

"Kate, yes. Kate." (A slow, amazed nod.) "Wow." He looked around. "How did she… how did you… How did you put it together that I knew your mom? Did she tell you? Is she here?"

"She's not here," I said. "She passed away a few months ago."

"Oh, gosh, I'm sorry to hear that," he said.

"It's okay. She was sick, and… it was her dying that led me here." I reached up near my own upper arm and touched Alex who was still wrapped around me. "I would have never met Alex or any of you guys if my mother wouldn't have led me here. I feel like my life has changed for the better, for sure."

"Aw, well, that's so nice," Ben said, being cordial but not getting it.

"This young lady is trying to tell you she's your daughter, Ben."

Ben's head whipped around to look at Ezekiel with a serious expression. "Whose? What? She. My? What? E, what? What are you saying? Are you messing with me? Is she mine?"

Ezekiel was smiling and nodding, and the two gentlemen stiffened-up physically and began pushing at each other like in a half-fighting celebratory dance that only brothers could pull off. They engaged in this for a few seconds. It made me want to giggle watching them.

Ben stepped back. "E. Seriously."

"I wouldn't lie to you about this," Ezekiel said.

And with no further hesitation, Ben let go of his brother and stepped to the side, positioning himself directly in front of me. He reached out for my arms, touching me ever so gently as he stared at my face. Alex was still behind me, but he loosened his grip. I wanted him to stay there, so I reached up and touched his arm again. Jude and Ezekiel said something to each other in an effort to give dad and I a moment.

"Is what he said true?" Ben asked, looking directly into my eyes.

I nodded. "All of it," I agreed. "I really am a writer, and I live in California. And I love Alex. And yes," I added. "Whatever time you spent with my mother resulted in me, apparently."

"She never told me," Ben said, staring at me with an amazed, regretful expression.

"She never told me, either," I said. "She never told anyone. Not even my dad, my other, Amos."

"How sure was she?" Ben asked.

"Positive," I said.

"I'm positive," Jude interjected. "She looks like Stella."

"And she sneezes ten times in a row like Livi," Ezekiel added.

"She looks like her mother," Ben said. "But I see what you mean about Stella. Livi, too, a little bit, in the eyes." Ben reached out and tentatively took me into his arms. He held me there, gradually hugging me tighter. "You are beautiful," he said, close to my ear. "An absolutely beautiful young woman. I'm proud of you, and I'm sorry I didn't get to know you before today." Ben pulled back, staring at me with tears in his eyes. It was just Ezekiel and Alex standing with us now. Jude had walked away. I saw him in the distance, talking to his wife. Ben stood there and took a good, long look at me. "Shoot, hot dang, you guys, I did good, didn't I?"

Ezekiel gave Ben two hardy pats on the back.

"She's pretty wonderful," Alex said. I had stepped away from Alex to hug Ben, but I turned back to him when he said that.

The Tanners were amazing, and I was overjoyed to have a new family who accepted me and loved me, but Alex was the best thing to come out of this.

He was my other half, my counterpart, my man. We had only known each other a short while, but I was completely changed. I blinked at Alex, making pretty eyes that only he could see, and he nudged his chin at me and looked at my mouth, which basically meant he wanted a kiss. I smiled and popped up leaning toward him, giving him a quick kiss.

"How did you meet my lovely daughter, Alex?" Ben asked when he saw that exchange.

My heart felt something when I heard him call me that. He sounded like he was proud to take ownership, which gave me a peaceful feeling.

"She was a landscaper," Ezekiel said, causing Ben's face to grow comically confused. "She was pretending," Ezekiel clarified. He put his hand on Ben's shoulder and pulled him toward the ballroom. "I'll explain while we walk," he said. He waved at Alex and me. "We'll meet you guys at the table in a little while. We'll have to talk about all of this more later. But I love you both. I mean that. This makes me happy, this whole situation. Welcome to the family."

Ezekiel was looking at me when he said that, and I smiled at him and gave him a little wave, holding the gesture while I glanced at Ben. They were both excited about the news, which made me happier than I thought it would.

I shifted to stare up at Alex when they walked away. "Oh, my goodness," I said breathlessly. "That was much easier than I thought it would be, actually.

I can't believe that just happened. I imagined him doing something dramatic demanding DNA tests."

"Did you really?"

"I didn't know what to think. I'm glad I didn't know he was here till the last minute, though, because I would have been freaking out all day leading up to it, and for no reason. He was so nice. And it was easy. It's a trip that he's here. I can't believe that just happened."

"Would you like to add to the wackiness of this moment?" Alex asked. He wore a serious deadpan expression, but I knew he was being light-hearted.

"Sure," I said with a shrug. "You got a dare for me or something?"

"Marry me," he said.

I pulled back and stared into Alex's dark eyes, my serious expression matching his. "Easy. Yes," I said. "And that's not wacky at all. That's the most normal thing that's happened to me all day." I was straight-faced when I said it, and Alex smiled at me.

"I mean it, though," he said.

"I definitely do, too," I agreed, letting a smile touch my lips. "Say the word, Alex."

"Word. Please."

"Yes," I said.

"So, that's it? We're getting married?"

I nodded staring blankly at him. "Yes. I think so. Yes."

"You think so, or you know so."

"I know so. I want to. I'm just, I just, I wanted to make sure you wanted to."

"I'm the one who asked you," he said.

"Then, yes," I said with a little shrug. "Any day."

"How about by spring?" he asked.

"If we can wait that long."

His smile broadened. "Do you think you'd be willing to move here?"

I nodded.

"Would you want to build a house on that lot?"

I nodded again.

"We have five magnolia trees in those woods," he said. "Jude went and counted and texted me about it this morning."

I snuggled up next to him. "The trees are just icing on the cake."

Epilogue

Six months later

I traveled back home to California several times during those first few months of our relationship, but Alex and I hated being apart and we did as little of it as possible.

Magnolia Borderlands got a movie deal, and I had just completed the first draft of the sequel. Alex had renegotiated his contract with UK, and he went from a twelve-month employee to a ten-month, giving him June and July off. We had just gotten married during the last week of May, so he took a week's vacation and now he was at the beginning of two full months off of work.

He deserved it. Tanner and the Wildcats basketball team had just finished an epic season, and Alex had been working overtime to keep them all healthy and in the game. I loved the sports aspect of his job. I had fun going to college games and hearing stories about the athletes from Alex.

We had been in California for five days now, and last night we had a party so we could celebrate our wedding with my California people. Alex and I had gotten married last week in a ceremony in Kentucky. We invited Amos, but I knew he wouldn't come. He did, however, come to our party in L.A., which was monumental for him.

He did a good job of accepting that I had met someone in Kentucky and fallen in love. I told him I would be moving there and that I was happy and his family had embraced me. I made sure Dad knew he was welcome to come visit me any time, although I knew he wouldn't. I would have to go to California when I wanted to see him.

Alex's family came from Iowa for the wedding, and Courtney and Gina came to Kentucky with me, but otherwise our wedding consisted of the Tanners and Alex's friends in Kentucky.

We had a ceremony of about eighty people, and Ben Tanner and his girlfriend, Sami, drove in from Philadelphia so he could walk me down the aisle. Olivia, my sister, came as well. I had met her at Christmas, and we had been in communication via text since. We were close by now, and it was great seeing her at the wedding.

I wasn't worried about hurting Amos. I knew he was in his own world over there in that Hollywood mansion. I could live my life openly in Kentucky, being honest about my biological father, and Amos would never find out.

I knew in my heart that I was doing the right thing by keeping it from him. I had done a lot of thinking and praying about it, and I realized that just because you knew the truth about something didn't mean you had to share it. Sometimes it was appropriate to carry a weight alone. It depended on whether or not the recipient of the news had anything to gain. With the situation we were in, Amos stood to gain nothing by knowing the truth. In this case, the truth would only hurt him. He understood and gave me his blessing when I told him I had met someone and was moving to Kentucky, and I felt that was all that needed to happen. Alex agreed with me, and both of us treated Amos like we knew nothing of my relationship to Ben Tanner.

Alex and I were at Amos's house now. We talked to the housekeeper for a few minutes. She said she was wrapping up and had already told my dad goodbye but that we could find him in his bedroom.

Alex had been here with me before, so none of this procedure was a surprise to him. My dad had a huge, gorgeous bed up on a platform, and he spent a lot of time in it. He had a little physical activity in his life. He had a home gym and a swimming pool, but when he was lounging, he was in his bed. He wasn't much of a couch or recliner man and he could rarely be seen in his living room at all. I definitely saw the housekeeper out there more than I did him.

Alex and I walked down the hallway till we got to Dad's bedroom. We knocked, and he called us in. He was on his bed just like I knew he would be. He was on top of the covers, wearing a robe and pajama pants with his hair standing on end. He used a remote to open the blinds a little more, letting light flood into the room.

"You need it like this in here all the time," I said, looking out at the patio through the wall of windows.

"I was about to take a nap," Amos said. "I was just about to close it all the way. I needed a good nap after you had me out partying all night."

I laughed as I crossed to his bed, jumping onto the end of it. "Thank you for coming," I said. "It meant a lot to us that you came."

"Yeah, thank you, Mister Rains," Alex said. He sat in a chair near the wall in my dad's room—the place where he had sat the last time he came in here.

"I'm happy for you two," Amos said. "I didn't want to miss it."

"You looked like you held up," I said, looking at Dad. "You stayed longer than I thought you would."

"An hour?"

"Yeah," I said. "That's a lot. Thank you for doing that."

"I had about six anxiety attacks, but it was a small price to pay to make it to my daughter's wedding."

I laughed. "Six? That's all? You can do six standing on your head."

He laughed, knowing it was the truth. Neither Alex nor I corrected Dad that it wasn't our actual wedding. He was choosing to ignore that, which I thought was sweet. It meant a lot to me that he even got out of the house.

"That hotel was nice," Amos said. "Patterson Place."

"It's awesome. That's where we're staying."

"I forgot you sold your apartment."

"Yeah, we've been in twice since then and stayed at that hotel. We love it. I noticed you brought Carlotta last night." I added. Carlotta was his housekeeper. She had accompanied him to the party.

"Yeah," he said. "I was glad she came. I wouldn't have been able to go alone. She drove and everything."

"We saw her just now when we got here."

"I thought she left," Dad said.

"She was on her way out. She's been coming here every day for ten years," I said.

"I know."

"Haven't you ever thought about just marrying her? Asking her if she wants to move in?"

"She wouldn't want to do that," Dad said.

"I'm actually sure she would," I said. "She loves you."

"You think?" Dad asked.

"Yes. I do. She's not just a housekeeper around here, if you haven't noticed. It would be great having her here. I wouldn't worry as much about you when I'm all the way across the country."

"That's fine with me if she wants to," Dad said a little too casually.

"You mean you'll marry her?" I asked.

He shrugged. "If she wants to, I don't see why not. She's here all the time, anyway. We're pretty much married as it is. I'll just ask her next time she's over here."

"Do you kiss her?" I asked, feeling shocked by his nonchalance.

"No."

"Then you're not pretty much married."

"Fine, I'll kiss her. Look, I thought you were coming for dinner tonight," Amos said. "It's only three o'clock. I was planning on having a nap." He used the remote to close the blinds a little, pushing us out.

I didn't mind. It wasn't meant to be offensive. That was just how he was.

"Alex and I came early. We're going to use your backyard. We'll either swim or use the hammock. We'll get some food delivered in a few hours, and I'll wake you up to come eat with us before we go."

"Okay," Dad said.

"You have to come out and eat with us," I said. "Like, in the kitchen. We're going hiking with Courtney tomorrow, so it'll be the last time I see you before we leave."

"I will. Just come wake me up in a few hours."

Alex and I left his bedroom. He finished closing the blinds on our way out, and the room was pitch black when we closed the door.

"Do you think he'll really marry Carlotta?" Alex asked as we walked through the house.

"I don't know," I said. "But I know she would be up for it, and I do think they'd be a good match. What do you want to do?" I asked, pulling him down the hall. "We have all afternoon. What do you want to do first?"

Alex chose the hammock.

It was an excellent choice.

My dad had gardeners and pool maintenance people, and his patio was well-kept. I used to think my dad's hammock was huge, but Alex did a good job of taking up most of it. I snuggled up next to him and we swayed silently for five or so minutes. I had no idea what he was thinking, and he had no idea what I was thinking. We just stayed there, resting together.

Finally, I leaned up positioning myself over him so that I didn't throw us off balance. Alex felt what I was trying to do, and he helped me, picking me up, pulling me across his chest. I leaned in and kissed him on the mouth simply because I could reach it and I couldn't resist. I loved the color of his mouth. It was barely darker around the edges, and I stared at his lips as I got closer.

We were newlyweds, and our mouths were constantly finding each other's. I loved the shape and the taste of his lips. I balanced my weight on him as we kissed. He had on shorts and a thin t-shirt, and I could feel his hard body through the thin layer of fabric.

I was in love with this man. It was the type of love where I thought about him when we weren't together and I felt all stirred-up inside when we touched. I smiled, thinking about how I had to go all the way to Kentucky to find a man like this.

He adjusted me, holding me securely. "What are you smiling at?"

"I'm just thinking about how big you are. How fitting it is that I found you at a horse farm."

"I'm feeling like maybe I should take offense to that," he said. He sounded serious, and he touched my side like he might tickle me.

I stiffened. "No, no, no, offense. I didn't mean to compare you to a horse, I just was thinking I don't think I could have found one like you in Los Angeles. Unless he was a Laker or something."

"You stay away from those Los Angeles Lakers," Alex said, acting serious, but teasing me. "They're up to no good."

"Well you need to stay away from… everybody who's not… me…" I said. I was hoping to come up with something wittier, but I got distracted, lost staring at his mouth.

"You want me to stay away from anyone who's not you?" he asked, his face cracking into a smile at how distracted I was.

"I want you to stay with me the most," I said, still absentmindedly staring at his mouth.

Alex's grin moved a little as he spoke.

I loved the sight of it.

"I will stay with you the most," he agreed. "I would love to stay with you the most."

"The most and forever?" I asked.

He held me near. "The most and forever."

The End
(till book 8)

Thanks to my team ~ Chris, Coda, Jan, Glenda, and Yvette